The Treasure Hunters Club
BOOK ONE

SECRETS
OF THE
MAGICAL
MEDALLIONS

The Treasure Hunters Club

BOOK ONE

SECRETS
OF THE
MAGICAL
MEDALLIONS

SEAN McCARTNEY

To Lori, who never stopped believing.

You are the love of my life.

Contents

ONE

A DIME IS STILL WORTH 10¢
Gunnison River—North Rim of Black Canyon, Colorado

THIRTEEN-YEAR-OLD TOMMY REED wore tan shorts and a blue T-shirt as he stood in the shallow part of the river. As the water moved slowly around his boots, his dark hair tasseled from the slight breeze coming through the canyon. His leather satchel hung around his neck, and he used his custom-made sifter to dredge through the mud.

His friend and fellow Club member Jackson Miller stood on the nearby bank of the river. "They are only dimes," Jackson said as he cleaned the spots of water from his glasses.

"That's true," replied Tommy, "but can you imagine how much they must be worth now?"

"Isn't this like the old joke about the two dollar bill? You know, 'how much is a two dollar bill worth?' And the answer is 'two dollars'?"

"Paper isn't silver." Tommy smiled at his friend. "You could be on your own like Chris or at home like Shannon. Besides, my Uncle Jack told me this is the best place to look for the dimes."

"Then why isn't he here?" Jackson asked.

1

"He's in Florida with his crew working on a Spanish Galleon."

"What's the story behind these dimes, anyway? Are you sure they're here?"

Tommy stepped out of the river, then pulled a rag from his leather satchel and dried his hands.

"In 1903, the Denver Mint sent six wooden kegs of dimes by wagon train to Phoenix. But there was a bad storm and the wagons never made it. They were lost somewhere between this canyon and Montrose."

"How do you know?" Jackson asked.

"Treasure hunters found the remains of four wagons around this area and a few dimes in the river."

"So if the dimes have been found, then why are we here?"

"They didn't find them all," Tommy said with a smile. "Legend has it that the bulk of the dimes were hidden from treasure hunters somewhere in the canyon."

"So you think we can find something that's been lost for over a hundred years?"

"Hey, are we the Treasure Hunters Club or what?"

"Most of the time it's 'what,'" Jackson teased.

"Just keep looking." Tommy bounded back into the river.

One mile up the canyon another treasure hunter—a darker, more sinister man—was looking for the same loot, but for different reasons. He watched as the teenagers dredged the river by hand.

"Young fools," he muttered to himself.

One of the three men working for him approached his side. "Boss, why are we following a bunch of kids?"

The man didn't answer. He just glared at his minion, then spit on the ground and rubbed it in with his boot.

"Keep on them, and don't ever question me again."

*   *   *

Chris Henderson stood beside a grove of old oak trees and scanned the area around the water's edge. He noticed a group of small stones stacked like a pyramid against a larger boulder. As the strongest and largest member of the Treasure Hunters Club, Chris usually performed his tasks solo, and today was no different.

Chris stared at the formation, studying it closely. *Looks manmade*, he thought as he ran toward the rocks.

From his position on a nearby hilltop, one of the men saw Chris and pulled out his walkie-talkie.

"A kid is running up the river," he said.

"Follow him."

*   *   *

The cellphone attached to Tommy's belt went off.

"Yes, Chris? You're kidding." He smiled. "We're on our way." Tommy closed the phone and turned to Jackson. "He found it."

Minutes later, Tommy and Jackson steered their canoes onto the shores of a small beach. They ran up to Chris, stopping when he flashed them a handful of dimes.

"Where did you find those?" Tommy asked.

3

"Hidden inside a small cave, surrounded by rocks. Strange thing was that when I found them they were all in neatly stacked boxes." Chris motioned for them to follow behind him. "You've got to see this." The boys walked for a bit until they spotted the rocks. "Move those stones and look for yourself," he said.

Tommy moved aside the small stones to reveal stacks of cigar-style boxes lined up in neat rows.

"I don't believe this."

"Why not?" Jackson asked.

"The dimes had to be scattered everywhere. This must be the work of more than one person."

"Didn't you say a group of treasure hunters found dimes by the river?" Jackson asked.

"Yeah," Tommy said, "but why hide them inside a small cave?"

Jackson thought for a minute. "Maybe a treasure hunter put them there for safekeeping and forgot where he hid them."

"Could be. But what kind of treasure hunter would do something like that?"

"A stupid one," a chilling voice answered from behind them.

The boys turned and saw an imposing man with lifeless eyes and a scruffy beard. He was flanked by three other men and wore a long black coat.

Tommy tried to see the man's face, but his features were hidden in shadows.

"Who are you?" Tommy asked.

"A real treasure hunter. Not like you and your pathetic Club."

"I don't think we're that bad," Chris said with a brief smile.

The man stared at Chris. "I think I'll be taking that treasure now."

"You can't do that," Tommy said.

"Who is going to stop me?"

"There are rules to treasure hunting."

"Which I could care less about. I'll bet you don't even know how much those dimes are worth."

"Um, ten cents?" Chris answered.

"Funny," the man said without a trace of laughter. "We're talking a million bucks and change."

"I think it would be more than that based on the melt-value of dimes," Jackson declared, quite proud of himself.

"So you're the smart one?"

Jackson shook his head no. It was a lie.

"Then shut up. This has taken up entirely too much time." The man motioned to his crew. "Start packing the boxes into the canoes."

"You're taking our canoes too?" Tommy said.

"Yes. Want to try and stop us?"

While the crew stacked the cigar boxes into two of the three canoes, Jackson leaned over to Tommy and whispered, "What do you want to do?"

"He's not going to take those dimes," Tommy said. "As soon as his men are done, we break for the boats."

Jackson nodded to Chris, who responded in kind.

"I'm sure you have already thought of this, uh, sir," said Jackson, "but with the extra weight of the dimes you're going to have a tough time navigating the canoes through the rapids."

"I thought you weren't smart?"

"I'm not. I just think you might have some trouble."

"We can handle it." The man's voice was cold.

One of the crew members approached the leader. "All the boxes are loaded, sir."

"See, now that wasn't so—" The man stopped mid-sentence as the Treasure Hunters Club sped past him, pushed the canoes into the water, and started rowing down the river.

"Get them!" he screamed.

Chris and Tommy paddled as fast as they could, Jackson right behind them.

"Tommy," Chris said between strokes. "Jackson is right. No matter how far ahead we get, we'll never make it past the rapids."

"Leave that to me," Tommy said.

Over his shoulder, Tommy saw the men climb into the last canoe and push off from the shore.

"We're almost to the rapids," Chris yelled. "You got a plan?"

Tommy pulled a rope from his satchel. "When we get close to one of those old oak stumps I'm going to throw the rope around it. That should hold us while those goons drift down river."

"What about Jackson?"

"I've got enough slack for him. But I'm going to need all of your strength for this one."

"No problem." Chris flexed his arms.

The canoes bounced against the force of the water as foam began to spill inside

"Anytime now," Chris yelled. "The current is getting stronger."

Tommy swung the rope and threw it toward an oak stump. As it wrapped around the stump, Tommy pulled hard.

"Hang on," he yelled to Chris and tossed him part of the rope.

When the rope's slack ran out, it tightened around the stump. The canoe hopped on the water as waves slammed against it and water flowed over the side.

"Tommy, we've lost some of the boxes." Chris's face was strained.

"Tommy," Jackson yelled from behind. "Throw me the rest of the rope."

Tommy released his right hand and felt the canoe slip a bit.

"I got it," Chris said. "Just get Jackson."

Tommy threw the rope toward Jackson, who caught it and then wrapped it around his forearm and braced himself.

The water carried the canoe a few more feet before it stopped. Jackson held the rope tightly as it tore into his palms. The water's speed increased, and Jackson screamed in pain.

"Hang on!" Tommy yelled over the fury of the foaming river.

The crew of men closed in on them. They reached out for Jackson's canoe, but the rush of waves pushed them away.

"Paddle back to them," their leader screamed as his men fought against the rapids.

"We can't," one of the crew called. "The water is too—" He never finished the sentence. The canoe capsized, dumping the men into the raging water.

The Treasure Hunters Club watched as the river broke the canoe into pieces. None of the men resurfaced.

"Okay, let's pull to shore," Tommy said.

"Tommy!" Jackson yelled. "The rope isn't going to hold!"

Tommy looked back and watched as the last thread of rope snapped and Jackson and his canoe drifted away.

"Jump," Tommy yelled. "I'll throw you more rope. Just jump!"

"But the dimes?"

"Forget about them." "Jump!"

Jackson closed his eyes and leapt into the raging waters. The current's angry hands grabbed him just as Tommy's rope bounced off his head.

Jackson blindly grabbed the lasso and wrapped it around his waist. Together, Chris and Tommy pulled him into the boat.

Jackson's canoe drifted aimlessly into the rapids, the boxes of dimes falling off along the way.

"Well, at least we have some of the dimes," Chris said.

"True," Tommy said. "Are you all right?"

As Jackson nodded, a rush of water tore off the back end of the canoe, taking with it the rest of the boxes.

"No!" Tommy shouted. He lunged for the last box, but it slipped from between his wet hands. He hit the floor with a thud, waking himself.

Tommy's head popped up and he stared at his digital clock.

4:15 a.m.

Great, he thought, *two more hours of sleep before school.*

Tommy lifted himself off the ground and fell back into bed. He closed his eyes and tried to sleep, but couldn't. Instead, his mind kept drifting to thoughts of treasure hunting. Tommy desperately wanted to get out of this town and travel the world looking for mankind's greatest treasures, like his uncle did.

When Tommy and his friends formed the Treasure Hunters Club in the sixth grade, they imagined the amazing trips they would take and the fabulous treasures they would find. In reality, they mostly sat around an old camper in Tommy's backyard and talked about treasure hunting. But Tommy was getting tired of that. He wanted adventure, excitement, something! Anything! He wondered when he and the Club would have their chance.

Tommy pulled the covers over his head, reminding himself that the hunt for dimes was just a dream. But a voice in the back of his mind kept asking: when would it become a reality?

TWO

THE TREASURE HUNTERS CLUB

TOMMY RAN HIS hand through his dark hair as he walked the aisles of the Mythological Artifacts Exhibit in awe. As a founding member of the Treasure Hunters Club, he made sure never to miss a chance to see real-world treasures, even if the artifacts were replicas.

"Tommy, the weapons are over here," Chris called.

Tommy walked toward the weapons exhibit and smiled with great satisfaction. The Mythological Artifacts Exhibit displayed the history of legendary treasure, along with information cards describing all the interesting facts of each item. The mythical originals of these fakes, Tommy thought, were once the obsession of every treasure hunter in the world based only on the rumor that they might exist.

Tommy stared at a nineteenth-century chief's axe: a long stick with a rock tied to it that belonged to the Oceanic god of the forests. There was an iron sword from Denmark, used by the Norse god Frey, with the ability to fight on its own. A large glass case displayed a bow and two arrows used by Diana, the Roman goddess of hunting. A suit of armor designed by Hephaestus for Achilles, the great Greek warrior, to protect him during war in Troy, hung in another case.

There was a weapon of great distinction showcased a few feet away in a special sealed-off section of the exhibit.

"Chris, look at this." Tommy pointed at the large case. "Thor's hammer." He stared at the mighty object.

The Norse god's hammer, the *Mjolnir*, never missed its target and always returned to Thor's hand whenever he threw it.

"It's fake," Chris said, unimpressed.

"So?" I'll bet centuries of treasure hunters searched for this."

Chris walked to another part of the exhibit while Tommy read every information card—some twice.

"What are these?" Chris asked, pointing at two brass objects suspended in the air.

"Those are *Vajras*," Tommy said. "Seventeenth century from Tibet, sometimes called the 'Thunderbolt Scepter.' Hindu gods Indra and Karttikeya used them as weapons."

"They threw them?"

"I guess." Tommy shrugged. "The Tibetans believed that those thunderbolts held magical powers to destroy evil forces."

"Do they?"

Tommy glanced at Chris. "They're fake, remember?"

"Oh yeah."

Tommy and Chris continued walking through the exhibit until they came across a table of medallions resting on a sheet of blue velvet. Tommy looked at the small cards next to each medallion, but before he could read any of them he was interrupted by a large man wearing a blue blazer. The Civic Center logo was stamped on his lapel.

"The exhibit will be closing in ten minutes," the man announced, "but the gift store will remain open for another hour."

"Come on," Chris said, "we've got a meeting."

Tommy took one last look around and decided he would come back to the exhibit when he had more time to study everything. The sun was beginning to set as he followed Chris outside to the bike rack.

"Can't wait to tell the others what we saw." Tommy unlocked the chain securing his bike.

"You know that Jackson will love the weapons," Chris said.

"So will Shannon." Tommy pushed on one of his pedals.

"She's a girl, God only knows what her reaction will be," Chris said as he got onto his bike.

*   *   *

The Treasure Hunters Club officially met once a week, but they still got together every day depending on what the group wanted to talk about.

Tommy and Chris turned their bikes down the Reeds' driveway, riding past the garage and into the backyard. An old camper sat near a large plot of land that was once used as an airfield, but now was overgrown with weeds and bushes. The camper had been left behind by the former owners of the house, so Tommy and his friends

13

turned it into their clubhouse. To the outside world the camper looked old, with chipped paint and rusty sides made it look old. But appearances were very deceiving. Using their talents, the four teens turned the decrepit-looking piece of metal into a treasure hunting fortress.

Tommy slid his coded key card through the lock. The green light granted him permission to open the door. When he walked into the old camper, Shannon and Jackson were already seated at a small round card table.

"You're late," Shannon barked as she threw a book onto the top of a shelf that stored many historical and archeological readings.

"We got held up at the exhibit," Tommy said with a smile.

"You got stuck looking at all the weapons, didn't you?"

Tommy tried to avoid making eye contact, but with Shannon it proved too difficult.

The two had lived on the same street since birth and had been friends since they could walk. Tommy only recently noticed how pretty Shannon's brown eyes were next to her sandy blond hair. She was taller than most of the boys, Tommy knew, and she feared no one.

"I like the weapons." Tommy took his seat.

"What did you see?" Jackson asked enthusiastically.

Jackson was, without a doubt, the smartest member of the Club. He tested out of every math level the middle school offered and was now taking advanced placement math at the new high school. For Jackson, the advanced placement classes offered a challenge, which was the one thing the young African-American man enjoyed more than anything else. But when it came to common sense and humor, Jackson seemed lost, often not getting the jokes. The Club members always teased him about having two last names, and it took him a while to realize that was true.

"Next time you can come with us," Tommy said to Jackson.

"Can we start?" Shannon asked.

"Yes." Tommy stood at the front of the table. "I call this meeting of the Treasure Hunters Club to order. All the members please say 'aye' if present."

Three "ayes" sounded loud and clear.

"Then we shall begin," Tommy said. "I would like to discuss the mystery behind the lost treasure of Harry Morgan. In 1671, after Morgan's buccaneers beat the Spanish in Panama, he supposedly hid the main part of the treasure from his men." Tommy noticed everyone starting to drift off, reminding him of his thoughts from the previous night. His fellow Club members were getting tired of doing nothing but talking about treasure hunting.

"Is this boring you guys?" he asked.

"Huh?" Chris broke from his trance.

"Come on, guys, pay attention."

They all apologized, but Tommy understood their feelings. Talking about treasure hunting didn't seem quite so exciting anymore.

"Speaking of Harry Morgan, how many ships have been lost in the Caribbean?" Jackson asked.

"Hundreds," Chris said. "Maybe thousands."

"And how many had loot on them?"

"Depends upon if they were a pirate ship or a Spanish galleon."

"I read that Spain was able to take most of the gold away before Morgan could get to it. Besides, it wasn't like the pirates kept good records or anything," Tommy said. "They were thieves and robbers."

"Like Captain Kidd?" Shannon said.

Tommy looked at her and shook his head.

"I'm just kidding, Tommy. We can't all be like your uncle."

"By the way, where is he right now?" Chris asked.

"Last email he sent said he was in Jamaica."

"You know where in Jamaica?" Jackson sat down at the computer. "Maybe we can find him."

"He'll send an email."

"I wish we could do what he does," Shannon sighed.

"So do I," Tommy said.

There was silence until Shannon asked, "Why don't we?"

"Why don't we what?" Chris asked.

"Set up a treasure hunt for ourselves."

"Where?" Tommy asked.

"Some place in the Caribbean."

"That's realistic." Chris shook his head.

"Why not?" Shannon looked offended. "You think we can't do it?"

"We can do the research part, Shannon," Chris said in an irritated voice, "but we can't go on a real hunt because we have no money."

Tommy nodded. "He's right. My uncle gets paid well to do these digs, especially since he's the best in the world."

A knock at the door startled the Club.

"Who is it?" Tommy yelled.

"Your dad," came a gruff reply. "Time for dinner, and your friends can't stay."

Jackson peeked out the window and saw Tommy's dad walking slowly back to the house. The math whiz turned to Tommy. "I don't get—"

"I know." Tommy nodded. "How can Uncle Jack, an adventurer and explorer, and my dad, a stiff, come from the same mother? I often ask myself the same thing."

"It's not his fault," Shannon said. "A lot of people are down after losing their jobs with this economy."

"He could be nicer," Tommy replied.

"We're outta here." Chris stepped outside and the other followed, waving goodbye.

Shannon stuck her head back through the door.

"He's not that bad, Tommy. He's just not your Uncle Jack."

"I know." Tommy smiled. "I'll see you in school."

When the door shut behind them, Tommy turned off the old computer. He made sure all the doors and windows were locked. As he made his way out the door, he glanced at the maps of the world and the United States

17

tacked on the wall. Tommy noticed all of the colored pins representing the treasure Uncle Jack had found. *So many*, he thought.

Just before he closed the door, he looked at the almost-empty treasure case with its many bare shelves. It held a few things sent from Uncle Jack, but not much else. Tommy frowned as he thought of all the times he and his friends had talked about filling the shelves with treasure of their own. *That's all it is*, Tommy thought. *Just talk.*

Tommy closed the clubhouse door and sulked into, as he often said, the house where dreams went to die to endure yet another dinner where his dad scowled and his mother cowered in fear.

"Why couldn't they get themselves together?" he wondered. As his Uncle Jack always said, "Just pull yourself up and start something new. Never let anything stand in the way of what you want."

Tommy sat down at the table and breathed slowly and deliberately. His mom, a cigarette dangling from her lips and her eyes swollen from crying, spooned potatoes and corn onto his plate before slicing off a piece of meatloaf.

Tommy's dad sucked down another beer and shot angry looks at his wife and son. Where, Tommy wondered, did all that hate come from? More importantly, why was it directed at him and his mother?

Tommy sat in silence and ate as he waited for the nightly explosion of anger that always accompanied a Reed family dinner.

THREE

DIAMOND JACK
Thirty miles off Port Royal Harbor, Jamaica

THE RESEARCH VESSEL *HANOJ* moved slowly over the Caribbean excavation site. The ship's captain was not paying much attention to the calm blue water as he sat transfixed by his computer screen's magnetic sounding charts.

Diamond Jack Reed did not look forty years old or, for that matter, much over thirty. Jack's rugged good looks and flair for drama belied his age. He was a man of strong convictions, the world's most sought after and famous treasure hunter. Treasure hunting made him extremely wealthy, although at first he didn't do it for the money. His charismatic charm and zeal wooed collectors and the press alike.

Jack Reed won his nickname by discovering the greatest diamond mine in the history of the world. Reed led an expedition into the deep jungles of the Congo to find another Hope Diamond, the most famous blue diamond in history.

Thanks to his unbelievable luck, Jack stumbled upon an entire blue diamond mine. Even though the Congo government denied excavation access to an American, the publicity Jack received catapulted him into the world of fame and money.

Using his newfound success, Diamond Jack assembled a team he called his "crew," who followed him around the globe on the hunt for more treasure.

Reed's incredible luck continued as he and his crew found a treasure off the coast of Oyster Bay, New York, believed to belong to the pirate Captain Kidd. The treasure's worth was estimated at thirty million dollars.

Other treasure hunters cursed Reed's magical touch and cringed when he and his crew made yet another one of the greatest discoveries of the twentieth century. Searching in West Central Mexico, Reed uncovered gold and jewels belonging to the Aztec Empire. Treasure hunters had searched for these artifacts for centuries, but only a man like Diamond Jack could find them.

Reed's reputation allowed him to pick and choose his hunts. When he found rare coins that didn't have much value to him, he sent them to his nephew Tommy.

Jack didn't have a wife, nor did he really want one, so he liked to think of Tommy as his own son. He didn't get along with Tommy's dad, but that didn't stop Jack from enjoying a good relationship with his nephew.

As he looked at grid charts in the *Hanoj* control room, Jack knew this current treasure hunt could be his last if he and his crew came through for their wealthy employer. The money generated would make them rich beyond their wildest dreams.

Then maybe he would settle down and take life easy for a change. Elizabeth might be the person to do that with.

Elizabeth Haden had worked with Jack for over ten years. She began her career as a starry-eyed dreamer and blossomed into one of the best treasure hunters on the crew.

She brought a woman's thoughts and ideas to their tasks, and Jack liked having her around. Though Elizabeth once told Jack he couldn't be someone's husband, she shared his passion for treasure hunting.

"How does it look?" Elizabeth asked as she came into the boat's navigation space.

"Hang on," Jack said, then turned to speak into a small microphone hooked up to a radio. "Have you got one, Shawn?"

"Yes, sir," Shawn's voice crackled over the speaker. "We got a hit at forty degrees off the starboard side."

"Roger that." Jack penciled in the hit on his grid paper.

He stared at his computer screen. Charts and maps lay on top of one another on his desk.

"What?" Jack finally asked Elizabeth.

"The magnetic survey," Elizabeth said. "Have we been able to narrow our search?"

"Yes. Shawn's done a great job and has found a major magnetic anomaly in this section of the water."

"Is it part of a larger wreck?"

"Doesn't matter. What we're looking for isn't going to be on a ship; we'll find it on the ocean floor."

"Jack," Elizabeth began, "the guys and I think it's time you told us exactly what we're looking for. You've never kept it a secret from us before this hunt."

Jack paused. "A special medallion."

"A medallion?"

"Yes."

"We are looking for a medallion from what time period?"

"Around the eighteenth century."

"You've got to be kidding." Elizabeth laughed. "Between the ocean currents, hurricanes, and everything else that goes on in these waters, you're telling me we've been out here for over a year looking for a needle in a haystack?"

"Have you lost faith, Elizabeth?"

"No," she stammered, "it's not that. But come on, Jack, you know how difficult finding such a small piece is going to be."

"I do," Reed acknowledged. "But I also know that I have found treasures others said were impossible or didn't even exist. Shawn's work on the magnetic survey and the work from the others on the mag vessel are making things easier. Besides, if we do this right, the site will make me super rich and I can retire." He unfolded another map and took out a pen. "You probably can too."

"What?"

"Retire when we find this medallion."

"I'm too young to retire," she said proudly.

"No one is too young to retire," Jack said.

"Why is this piece so important?"

"I'm not sure. Our employer desperately wants it. I figured by making my fee ridiculously high he'd give up, but he said it was no problem, so now I'm on board. Truthfully, I've seen so many different medallions lifted from these sea floors that I find it hard to differentiate between any of them."

"What's so special about this one?"

"It's supposed to be made of gold and have some sort of blue stone engraved in the middle."

"With over three hundred years in salt water, that stone might not be there anymore."

"I told our guy that, but he didn't seem to mind."

"What's his name? Is he a collector?"

"Manuel de la Ernesto, and he might be a collector." Reed shrugged. "I didn't ask."

Matt Stone, a young man new to Jack's crew, entered the control room wearing scuba diving gear.

"Jack, we are ready to dredge the area"

Reed nodded. "Good. Make sure the pumps are okay and you and Shawn can go down."

"Will do," Matt said, and then left.

"Were you able to fix the water-fed dredges?" Elizabeth asked, forgetting about her and Jack's discussion.

"Yeah," Jack answered. "Took a bit of doing, but we managed."

"So you're using both pumps?"

"For what we're being paid, I would vacuum the floor of the entire Atlantic Ocean if I had to." Jack said with a smile.

Elizabeth frowned and looked at him strangely. "This isn't just for the money, is it, Jack?"

Reed stopped looking at his charts and turned to his most prized pupil. His blue eyes beamed. "No, it's always about the chase; solving the puzzle. If we can make some money in the process, then so much the better."

Elizabeth smiled in relief. "Good. I'll go help the rest of the crew."

Jack hoped she believed his lie. He didn't like to talk about his feelings, and though he could imagine the end of his career, he didn't want to admit it to anyone.

Diamond Jack Reed returned to his charts, but in the back of his mind he imagined retiring in comfort. The thrill that kept him on the chase for so many years had faded for the hunter, and these days he had to look harder for inspiration.

As he stared at the maps, maybe, he feared, neither inspiration nor the medallion was out there anymore.

FOUR

AT SCHOOL

KENNEDY MIDDLE SCHOOL SAT on the eastern part of town and held over eight hundred students in grades six through eight. Kennedy paired with another middle school on the west side of town to funnel students into the already crowded and newly built Ronald Reagan High School.

As an eighth grader, Tommy felt an incredible urge to move on to high school.

Tommy never considered himself the most popular kid at Kennedy. He fit into the niche of quiet students who worked for good grades. His friends, with the exception super smart Jackson, were the same. Teachers never worried about them turning in assignments because they always did.

"It's not that hard," Shannon always said.

While grades never worried Tommy, walking the hallways during class changes did. A student named Zachary Butler terrified Tommy and many others.

Zach, the class bully, had a large body, thick hair, dark eyes, and a bad attitude. He'd repeated the eighth grade so many times rumor had it that he was given his own parking space in the teacher's lot. Like a shark sensing a wounded fish, Butler zeroed in on Tommy during the switch to Language Arts class.

"Tommy," Zach said, grabbing Tommy by the back of the shirt.

Tommy felt his heart leap. "Yeah, Zach." Tommy turned to the man-child.

"I didn't bring my lunch today."

"That's too bad."

"I was thinking you could help me with that."

"How?"

"By giving me yours."

Tommy smiled. "I didn't pack a lunch. I'm buying the school lunch."

"That's good. I can just take your money then."

"You're taking my lunch money?" Tommy said, aghast. "Isn't that a little cliché? I mean, come on, Zach. It's the twenty-first century. You can't think of anything better than taking someone's lunch money?"

Zach thought for a moment, clearly stuck on the word cliché, before finally saying, "I could just start punching you in the face."

Tommy raised his eyebrows. "Okay, not really what I had in mind."

"Then give me what I asked for." Zach pulled Tommy closer to him.

"Hey, what's the problem?"

Tommy looked up to see Shannon walking toward them.

"Zach, what are you doing? Let him go, or else you and I are going to have a problem."

Zach released Tommy from his grasp and stared at Shannon.

Tommy straightened his shirt, whispered, "Thank you," to Shannon, and walked away.

"No problem," Shannon said in a proud voice and turned to Zach. "Stop giving me your tough guy stare. I don't buy it. But if you're feeling froggy, go ahead and jump. I smacked you down before and I don't mind doing it again."

Zach didn't move. For all his bravado, he could not deal with Shannon McDougal. Not only did she stand a full head taller than him, but when they were younger she would also routinely beat him up for picking on smaller kids. When she wasn't around, Zach could dominate a room; but if she was, he'd slink into a corner and hide. For this and many other reasons, Tommy enjoyed having Shannon in the Treasure Hunters Club.

As the end of the day neared, Tommy walked into his last and favorite class, Mr. Crist's Social Studies. Tommy, who had learned the value of history from his Uncle Jack, always enjoyed the lessons, even if some of his classmates did not.

He saw the video set-up and wondered what selection Mr. Crist had pulled from his ever-expanding DVD collection.

Eventually the dark lights and soft documentary voice lulled Tommy into a stupor. Unfortunately for the class, Mr. Crist handed out a question sheet that went along with the movie. And, of course, it was for a grade.

The movie, which came from a History Channel program called *History's Mysteries*, contained stories about lost ships and their treasures.

Though interested in the topic, after the first twenty minutes Tommy felt his eyes droop and his head tilt back. He couldn't stay awake. He tried to refocus on the movie, but his eyes became too heavy. Finally the narrator caught his attention, and he shook his head and blinked several times.

"In 1712, one of the worst, most violent hurricanes swept through the Port Royal Harbor in Jamaica, destroying over thirty-eight ships believed to be carrying millions of dollars in coins, jewelry, and silver."

The narrator continued speaking, but Tommy drifted off again. His mind wandered to a recent email from his uncle. Tommy remembered he was in Port Royal. He hoped Uncle Jack would send him something from his excavation.

Tommy closed his eyes and pictured himself on a ship discovering buried treasure, his friends right by his side. The dream recurred often, and Tommy longed for the day when he would be a real treasure hunter.

Tommy watched the final moments of the video showing the devastating effects of a hurricane on wooden ships. He cringed at the destruction.

As the video ended, Tommy wrote his name on the question sheet and turned it in to Mr. Crist.

Tommy kept his dream alive that someday he would be out on the seas just like his uncle, finding lost treasure and gaining fame for every discovery.

✻   ✻   ✻

The buses spewed smoke as they waited behind the school building for the students of Kennedy to come pouring out. The administration staggered the dismissal times so the younger students could board the buses first.

Finding a seat on the bus wasn't a problem for Tommy. The problem, from his view, was avoiding Zach Butler. Several times during the year, the oversized eighth grader caused Tommy to miss his bus. One time Zach sat on him, and another time he stole Tommy's book bag. Shannon got it back immediately, but that didn't make Tommy feel any safer.

Tommy wanted to blend in with the crowd and avoid Butler completely.

Mr. Crist dismissed the class. Tommy sprinted to his locker, grabbed his books, and quickly headed for the stairs. He started down and then stopped.

Zach stood at the bottom, looking like a lion ready to pounce. Tommy turned around and started to climb back up when Chris and Jackson appeared.

"Let's go," Jackson said, smiling.

"Wrong way, dude," Chris added.

"Look." Tommy pointed toward Zach.

The boys didn't move.

"Shannon is at gymnastics," Jackson said.

"We don't need her." Chris's voice was confident.

"Yes we do," Tommy said.

After a long pause, Chris began walking back down the stairs. "Screw this. I'm going."

Watching their friend's courage did little to help Jackson and Tommy feel up to the task, but they followed him anyway.

A pack of seventh grade girls started down the steps at the same time, and the boys fell in line with them. They had just passed Zach when his voice rang out, "Reed, I'm coming after you!"

Tommy slammed into one of the girls and they both fell to the ground. Her scream caused the other girls to squeal and laugh, but Zach continued his pursuit.

Chris and Jackson tried to step in front of the massive boy, but Zach bowled them over.

Jackson looked at Chris. "I thought you had him?"

"I thought you did," Chris said.

"Forget it now because he's about to kill Tommy."

Tommy scrambled to his feet and ran toward the door. All he had to do was make it to where his bus was waiting outside. Five steps away, he told himself, and then he saw Zach step in front of the open door. His arms were crossed, his legs were spread, and the look on his face said, "Gotcha."

Without thinking, Tommy ran at the building-sized boy. At the last second, he slid under Zach's legs like a baseball player coming into home plate and disappeared out the door.

By the time Zach turned around, Tommy had already stepped onto his bus. Chris and Jackson went through a different door and joined Tommy.

As the bus pulled away, the three boys watched Zach stomp his feet in anger at missing his prey.

Tommy looked at his friends and breathed a sigh of relief. "We need a plan for dealing with him. Someday either he's going to get us, or else we're going to have to get him."

"He's bound to get into trouble," Chris said.

"Chris is right," Jackson agreed. "I mean, the kid is what, thirty? Thirty-one?"

"Maybe we could get him on child abuse charges or endangering a minor?" Tommy laughed.

"That is definitely our next step," Chris said.

FIVE

DISCOVERY

MATT STONE HELPED SHAWN Dawkins, one of
Jack's top crewmen, place the artifacts from the dredge into
large water tanks.

"What's next?" Matt asked.

Though Matt was young, he impressed the others
with his strong work ethic as he learned the ropes of
working an excavation site on a treasure hunt.

"We start the reverse electro-analysis," Shawn said.

"Wouldn't a pick ax or acid work faster?"

Shawn laughed. "If we want the artifacts destroyed,
we'll use your method. Mel Fisher developed reverse electro-
analysis for the specific purpose of cleaning ancient artifacts.
See, the process separates oxygen molecules from the rust
deposits that have caked on the sunken relics.

"When artifacts are excavated from the bottom of
the ocean, they are encrusted with coral concretion.
Organisms attach themselves to the artifact and die, leaving
skeletal remains as hard as concrete. Conservation is the
process of stabilizing and protecting artifacts from further
deterioration using specific treatments. The goal is to
preserve the artifact."

"How long will this take?" Matt asked.

"The treatment process can take a few hours or a few years, depending on the material. The stuff we are looking for shouldn't take long at all."

Matt stared into the large tanks. "Wow, look at all of this stuff. Looks disgusting with the residue coming off of them."

"We've got to make sure to keep the artifacts wet. If they are exposed to air before the treatment is complete, their physical and chemical state will be altered."

"What year are these from?" Matt pointed to a set of recently cleaned coins.

"Probably the eighteenth century, stolen by pirates," Shawn said.

It took a while, but Dawkins eventually pulled six medallions from the cleaning. Two were still intact, the other four chipped and broken.

"That's what we're looking for." Shawn held the medallions in his hand. "Call Jack."

"These don't look very good," Matt said.

"I'll clean up the ones that are salvageable and the rest we'll throw away."

Matt made the call to Reed.

"He's coming." Matt watched Shawn begin the cleaning process. "I thought there was only supposed to be one medallion."

"When it comes to excavating," Shawn said, "you never know what you're going to find."

☆   ☆   ☆

33

An excited Jack arrived in the conservation room with Elizabeth in tow. "Where is it?" he asked.

"Actually, Skip, there were six medallions. Four were worthless, all smashed up, but two of them are intact and look pretty good," Dawkins said.

"Two?"

"Yeah."

"What did you do with the other four?" Elizabeth asked.

Shawn pulled out a plastic bin and showed them the broken medallions. They all agreed they were not worth keeping.

"Which one has a blue stone in the middle?" Jack asked.

"Both do."

"Let me see that." Jack looked at each medallion carefully, turning them over in his hands for several seconds before handing them back to Shawn.

"Well?" Elizabeth asked.

"Well what?" the famous treasure hunter said.

"Do you know which one he wants?"

"I'm thinking the one with the Spanish markings, since Manuel is Spanish."

"Or claims to be," Elizabeth said. "You know, Jack, through all of my research the name Ernesto doesn't come up at all. I don't think he is who he says he is."

"His checks clear," Jack said with a smile and a wink.

Elizabeth looked exasperated. "All right then, where are the other markings from?"

"Don't know," Jack said. "They are unlike anything I've ever seen before, and I've seen a lot."

Elizabeth grabbed the medallions from Jack. She carefully studied the one with the strange markings.

"Seems like a form of hieroglyphics, but these markings don't look like pictures, more like symbols. Are you thinking eighteenth century?"

"Maybe," Jack said. "Shawn, run this through the computer. Then we can make a definitive choice."

Jack studied the medallion with the unusual markings more closely. "I don't think this is the one. And if it isn't, I'm going to send it to Tommy. I haven't sent him anything good lately."

"That's your brother's kid?" Shawn asked.

"Yeah." Jack smiled. "Great kid, but a lousy home life. Here, take these to the lab and see what you can find out."

"No problem." Shawn left, Matt following behind.

Jack shook his head. "I never could understand my brother."

"Wouldn't he say the same thing about you?" Elizabeth asked.

Jack thought for a moment. "Probably."

"I don't get it. What is it that you two can't stand about each other?"

Jack shrugged. "I really don't know, but we've always been different."

He sat down at a desk and placed his hands on the table.

"You know," he began. "My brother was always a step behind me, and to be honest I think it was by choice. When we were in high school he always got in trouble over the dumbest things, and I never did. After we graduated, I wanted to backpack through Europe, but he refused. He got a job six months out of junior college and married soon after.

"She was nice, but young, you know, like she thought my brother was something he really wasn't . . . like rich. When I left home at nineteen, I didn't look back. I sent cards and videos to my brother and mother, but never saw a reason to spend much time there.

"Then Tommy came along, and boy did I like that kid. I see him a couple of times a year, send him emails, and talk on the phone now and then. He seems like he has a lot on the ball. It's like he inherited all of the good parts of my brother and his wife, and none of the bad."

"Maybe you should think about seeing your brother," Elizabeth said. "What does he do now?"

"Sits around and complains about life, mostly. Just before Mom died, she told me he lost his job and then got fat, smoked and drank too much, and became a deadbeat. Life dealt him bad cards, and he didn't play them well."

"That's sad," Elizabeth said.

Jack seemed lost in thought. "Sure is."

Shawn returned from the computer lab. "Still nothing?" Jack asked.

36

"We found a bunch of sites about ancient hoaxes and fake treasure." Shawn shook his head. "Stuff we've seen before that has no validity. Matt is pretty good when it comes to research. He'll find out what those markings are, or maybe it's just a piece of junk?" He laughed and left the room.

Jack smiled and stood up. "All right then, call Manuel de la Ernesto and tell him we have found his medallion with the blue stone."

"You still want to send the other one to your nephew?" Shawn asked.

Jack thought for a moment. "Yeah, I think he'd like it." The treasure hunter then turned to Elizabeth. "Maybe it can bring some good luck to his life."

She smiled and nodded her approval. "Maybe."

SIX

TREASURE MEETING

TOMMY WALKED SLOWLY UP the steps to his front
door. His backpack hung off his right shoulder, and he set it
down in the doorway without a sound.

When he entered the house, his father was snoring
loudly on the couch while his mother stood in the kitchen
sniffling over a mixing bowl as she used a spoon to stir
something.

"Hey, Mom," Tommy whispered, careful not to
wake his dad.

His mom smiled back at him weakly. "Hi, honey,
how was your day?"

"Good. Mom, are you okay?"

"Sure," she said as the tear stains on her cheeks
cracked. "Everything is great."

Tommy felt helpless. He wanted to comfort her,
but didn't know how. He wondered how his family seemed
to have fallen so far off track.

"I'll be out in the clubhouse."

His mom nodded. "Fine."

Before he went out the back door, Tommy asked,
"Are you sure you're going to be all right?"

His mom breathed in deeply. "Yeah." They both shuddered when they heard the snorer move. "Yeah," she reiterated. "I'll be fine. You go."

Shannon clicked the computer mouse several times before she got to the Internet. She wasted no time working her way to the website she wanted and began reading.

"Next time find me, and I'll come and get that buffoon off you guys," she said, continuing to stare at the computer screen.

The three boys sat at the conference table, looking at one another and shaking their heads. Each one hated the fact that they needed a girl to help them with Zach.

"Shannon," Chris said. "What did you do to Zach? I mean, do you have naked pictures of him or something?"

She laughed and shook her head. "No, I used to beat him up when we were kids. I think he knows I could still kick his butt, so he avoids me."

"I think he likes you," Jackson said. "That's the only explanation for why he never raises a fist to you."

Shannon turned away from the computer screen and glared at Jackson. "Whether he likes me or not is irrelevant, because he knows I could whip him. And you should talk! I don't recall you ever raising a fist ever."

Jackson looked at Chris and Tommy, who nodded.

"She's right," Tommy said.

"Yeah," Chris chimed in. "You never do."

Jackson started to fume. "Can we get this meeting going?"

"Sure," Tommy said. "Shannon, let's go."

Shannon clicked off the site, walked slowly to the round table, and flopped into a seat.

"So what are we going to talk about today?" she asked.

"I want to discuss the prospect of going on an expedition," Tommy announced.

The Club members gave him a blank stare.

"Tommy, we've been over this," Chris said. "We don't have any money."

"And we aren't going to get any," Jackson added.

Tommy nodded. "I understand that. All I'm saying is, let's plan an expedition as if we had money."

"Then we'd go," Shannon said.

"Good. Where should we go?"

"The Caribbean," Jackson said.

"Why?" Chris looked at him.

"Think of the amount of gold lost there because of pirates and smugglers during the late eighteenth and nineteenth centuries. And it's sitting at the bottom of the ocean." Jackson shook his head. "It could be worth millions."

"We could rent a charter boat and get all the scuba equipment." Tommy grew excited. "And then we could go down to the Straits of Florida and the Caribbean Sea to check out areas for lost treasures. We could make a fortune and be real treasure hunters like my Uncle Jack."

No one spoke for a moment as they daydreamed about the impossible.

"Too bad it's never going to happen," Jackson said, bringing the dream to an end.

"It could." Tommy tried to revive the vision.

"Tommy," Shannon said. "I know that you want us to be real treasure hunters, but the truth is we are just kids from a small town who meet to talk about treasure hunting. We've never actually done it."

"I have too," Tommy protested.

Shannon looked at him. "Tommy, going out with a metal detector and finding an ancient soda can is not treasure hunting."

"But it was a TAB! I don't even think they make those anymore."

"Isn't that the soda in the pink can?" Chris asked.

"Pink?" Jackson looked disgusted. "Who would ever use a pink can?"

"My mom used to drink it when she would diet," Chris said.

"But your mom is skinny."

Chris shook his head. "She is now."

"Enough of this!" Shannon screamed. "My God, you guys get off track so easily."

She turned to Tommy. "Treasure hunting is going to have to wait for us. I'm sorry."

Tommy looked at the ground. "I know you're right," he said. "I just think the only way out of this place, this house, this town, is through treasure hunting. It's how my uncle got out, and he has a crew, like you guys." Tommy shook his head. "I guess it's pointless. Maybe we should just end this Club."

"Wait a minute!" Chris stared at him. "We aren't going to do that. We can still talk about things we'd like to find and where they might be."

"He's right," Jackson said. "Then we could gather information about them and decide what we would do to find the treasure if we had money. Maybe even talk to your uncle for some help or ideas."

"Yeah, sure. Maybe. Then what would we look for?"

"How about the Beale Treasure?" Chris said. "Or Noah's Ark?"

"Noah's Ark?" Jackson repeated. "It was made of wood. I'm sure it has already rotted."

"You don't think it was made of gold?" Chris asked.

Jackson waved off his friend and looked at Tommy. "We could see if those creatures we read about are really alive, like the Kongamato, the lizard bird, or the Olitiau, that bat creature in Cameroon."

"They're right," Shannon said. "We don't have to end the Club because we can't go on treasure hunts. We'll just have to do it right here in the confines of the club house."

"You guys still want to do that?" Tommy looked at his friends.

"Beats going home," Jackson said.

"Besides, this will be good preparation for high school when we have to do research papers and stuff. And you never know, things might change," Shannon said.

"I appreciate all that you guys are doing, but we're just stuck in this small town and nothing is going to happen until we leave it."

"Oh, stop that," Shannon said to Tommy. "I told you, things can change—It'll just be later, that's all."

"No." Tommy's shoulders slumped. "I won't stop. I mean, my parents are a mess. How can I beat that?"

"Through hard work," Shannon said.

"I could leave and they might never know. Probably wouldn't even care."

"Bull. That's a lie," Jackson said.

"Ever see my dad?"

Jackson nodded. "Okay, you've got a point, but that doesn't mean you leave."

"Jackson's right, Tommy," Chris said. "Quit feeling sorry for yourself." He paused, unsure how his friend might respond to his criticism. "Your Uncle Jack wouldn't do it."

Tommy slumped in his chair. "I know. I just really want to be a treasure hunter, and the possibilities aren't looking very good because I'm here."

"Don't be so sure," Jackson said. "You never know when something will happen to change your life."

SEVEN

MONEY MAN

JACK AND ELIZABETH SAT at a secluded table near
the back of the restaurant and waited for Manuel to arrive.
Rain drove most of the patio diners inside, though two
younger couples stayed outdoors drinking Sangria and
getting soaked. The restaurant's specialty was jerk chicken
and fried potatoes, a dish that became Jack's favorite after
spending more than a year working near Jamaica.

"How old is Mr. Ernesto?" Elizabeth asked.

"Don't know." Jack looked toward the doorway.

"He's from where? Spain?"

"Never asked."

"You never asked?"

"No, it never came up."

"I've got to say that I have never heard of a famous
Ernesto family. What are they royalty of, Europe or South
America?"

"I don't know." Jack shrugged.

The waiter came to the table.

"Two Tings please," Jack said. He turned his
attention back to Elizabeth. "He pays us a lot of money."

"Is that all you worry about?"

"Liz, I would love to tell you that we are searching for something that will help mankind better understand history, but unfortunately we are doing this for a ton of cash."

"I'm surprised at you, Jack." Elizabeth smiled at the waiter as he put two bottles of Ting, Jamaica's famous grapefruit soda, on the table.

"Why?"

"Because when I first started, you told me that treasure hunting was meant to clarify, understand, and, in a way, touch history."

"You also have to live, my dear. When it's this much money, we'll clarify history later." Jack looked up. "There he is." He waved his hand.

Elizabeth turned to see an older gentleman, probably in his late fifties, wearing a tan shirt and matching pants. He looked like a young grandfather, but something about him didn't sit well with Elizabeth. He used a handkerchief to wipe the rain—*or was it sweat?* Elizabeth wondered—from his brow.

"Be nice," Jack warned as he stood up. "Don't say anything about the medallion. I want it to be a surprise. Manuel, over here."

Manuel de la Ernesto walked toward their table. He was followed by two large men with no necks and large bodies.

"Jack, so good to see you again." Manuel pulled a chair out from the table.

"Manuel, this is my top assistant, Elizabeth Haden."

Manuel smiled at her before sitting down. "Such beauty." He grabbed her hand and kissed it gently.

"Charming," Elizabeth said, unimpressed.

"What can I get you?" Jack asked.

"Ting will be fine."

Jack motioned to the waiter.

"Do they need anything?" Jack glanced at the other men.

"They are all right."

"You must be pretty important to have two bodyguards," Elizabeth said.

Manuel waved her off with a smile.

"Now, Jack, tell me how it's going and what my money is buying me."

"We had a good week," Jack began, taking a sip of his drink. "We dredged over two miles of grid area and hauled in a ton of stuff."

"Jack, I have spent a lot of money to get this medallion back into my family."

"I know. And you have been very generous with this expedition, which makes this announcement that much harder." Jack tried to hold back his grin.

Manuel eyed Jack. "What do you mean by 'harder'?"

"We found it!" Jack took a long swig of his drink.

Manuel's eyes lit up. "You are the best," he said, and raised his glass. "To Diamond Jack, the greatest treasure hunter of all time!" He gulped back his soda.

Jack gave a weak smile and sipped his drink. "Thank you, Manuel. When we're done with our reverse electro-analysis, you will have a clean artifact."

"I am sorry for my ignorance, but what is reverse electro-analysis?"

"A way to clean the artifacts," Jack said. "But if, as you've said, the medallion is made of gold, then it won't be harmed."

"Why not?"

"Because gold is impervious to the elements underwater, even after centuries on the ocean floor."

Manuel looked at Jack strangely. "But what of the gem in the middle?"

"That's why it will need cleaning."

"And how long does this reverse thing take?"

"Depends on the size of the artifact, how old it is, and how much debris is on it."

Elizabeth waited for a lull in the conversation before speaking. "Mr. Ernesto, why is this artifact so important to your family?"

A cellphone rang, and Manuel pulled the slender object from his pocket. "Yes." He listened to the voice on the other end of the line, his cheery expression never changing. After a moment, he held his hand to cover the phone. "I must take this. Please excuse me."

Manuel got up from the table and walked to the front door while talking quietly into his phone. His two bodyguards followed behind.

Jack smiled as Elizabeth frowned.

47

"What?" he asked.

"Jack." She shook her head. "You trust this guy?"

"I don't need to trust him as long as his checks clear. Look how happy he is that we found that medallion," Jack said as he admired Manuel.

"Yeah, almost too happy."

"What does that mean?"

"It means there's something strange about this guy. I mean, he's got those two huge monsters that follow him and he never answers a question straight. Don't you see that?"

"No, I don't!"

"All right then," Elizabeth said.

Manuel walked back to the table with a smile. "Business never takes time off. So when can I get my medallion?"

"Mr. Ernesto," Elizabeth began.

"Please call me Manuel."

"Manuel, we were interrupted by your call, but I was wondering what is so special about this medallion? You've spent a lot of money on the expedition. Is it really worth that much?"

"I have collected jewels and artifacts from all over the globe that once belonged to my family. I am the last of the Ernesto clan and I want to keep my name and my heritage alive," he said. "Look at this." He pulled out a medallion the size of his hand and showed it to Elizabeth. There was a red stone in the middle. "I had this recovered from the Straits of Florida, and through exhausting research found that another medallion of this exact size, only with a blue stone, is out there."

Elizabeth studied the medallion, noticing that the outside was smooth and had no markings, unlike the ones they had found. She handed the medallion back to Manuel.

"Then why is this so important?"

"Many people believe that medallions have, how would you say, magical powers, Ms. Haden."

"That's why you want these medallions? For their magical abilities?"

Manuel laughed. "Of course not. Their value separately is worth nothing. But together their worth would rise considerably."

Elizabeth looked at Jack. "So it is all about the money."

"No, my dear. This one," he said as he held up the medallion, "means something special to the Ernesto family, and now with your help we have a complete set for my collection. When I am gone, I will donate all of my treasures to museums and the family name will live on forever."

"Where is your family from?" Elizabeth asked.

"All over, really. Classic nomads, the Ernestos. We have settled in many places."

"Where exactly?" she pressed.

Manuel smiled, ignoring the question, and turned to Jack. "I would like to see the medallion."

"We will," Jack said, "but how about some dinner first?"

"Excellent idea," Manuel replied. "The dinner will be on me as a great celebration."

Jack smiled at Elizabeth, who didn't return the gesture.

After dinner, Elizabeth got into Jack's rented car. "I don't care what you say," she said, "but there is more to this Ernesto family than he is telling us. Did you see the way he avoided the question about his family origins? Strange."

"Don't worry about it, Elizabeth. Some people are just private. I wouldn't share my family's sad history."

Elizabeth didn't seem satisfied. "No medallion is worth that much, and his talk about magical powers was creepy."

"Until you find out something different, let's give him the medallion and be done with it, though I will miss the jerk chicken." Jack smiled at her.

"So you don't mind if I do some checking around?"

"Do your best." Jack shifted the car into gear.

"I plan to," Elizabeth said, her mind already working.

Once on the boat, Manuel could barely contain his joy as he held the medallion in his hand like a mother cradling a newborn. He turned it over, admiring the blue stone.

"You really are the best," he said to Jack.

Jack smiled. "Just doing what I was paid to do, and I had a lot of help."

"You are too modest."

"Manuel, just so you know, we found—"

Manuel interrupted. "Jack, I really can't thank you enough for what you have done. The medallion is finally back where it belongs: with the Ernesto family."

"Yeah," Jack agreed, "but like I was saying, we also found some jewels and old coins that are worth quite a bit. Maybe you would be interested in them?"

"You keep them." Manuel's eyes never left the medallion.

Elizabeth seemed surprised. "Mr. Ernesto," she began, only to be interrupted.

"Please call me Manuel," he insisted.

"I'm so sorry, Manuel, but Jack is right. We found many good pieces, not just the jewels and coins."

Manuel waved her off. "I said for you to keep them. A gift from me to you, eh?"

Manuel rubbed the medallion with his thumbs and looked at Jack. "This was worth every penny I spent."

"I'm glad," Jack replied. "I must say, getting the money was pretty good too."

Everyone in the wheel room laughed.

Shawn Dawkins entered and seemed surprised by the number of people in the room.

"I'm sorry," he said. "I didn't know anyone was meeting here."

"No problem," Jack said. "Manuel de la Ernesto, meet one of my other fine crewmembers, Mr. Shawn Dawkins. He's actually too young to be this good and, thankfully, doesn't have a strong enough memory to remember when I was."

"Pleasure to meet you." The young man extended his hand.

"Likewise." Manuel shook Shawn's hand.

"Shawn is the main reason we found such a large cache. He was the leader of the dive and the main dredge operator at the bottom of the harbor."

"Then I should send him the check?" Manuel asked with a grin.

Jack laughed then with a mock-serious expression said, "You are kidding, right?"

Manuel laughed out loud again. "Oh, Jack, we need a drink. Get us some champagne." Manuel looked at the medallion, studying it more carefully. His eyes narrowed. "These markings are Spanish?"

"What?" Jack leaned in for a closer look. "Those? Oh, yeah. To make sure they were a literal translation, we ran them through the computer, and it reads ... here, let me see that printout." Jack grabbed a sheet of paper from Elizabeth.

She translated before Jack could read the paper. "It reads, 'light into dark,' and the other side says, 'dark into light.' But I am sure you knew that, Manuel."

Manuel smiled weakly and nodded. Elizabeth studied the old man's face. "Do you know what it means?"

Manuel shifted uneasily before he spoke. "Long ago, there was a battle over control of light and dark magic. The two groups involved were the Dorcha, followers of the dark magic, and the Leois, who followed the light. The Dorcha believed in combining the powers of light and dark, but the Leois felt that all that power in one place was too much for one person and wanted the two separated. The Leois were able to use a band of gypsies to place the power of light and dark magic into two medallions to safeguard."

"Now you have them both?" Elizabeth asked.

"Yes, I do." Manuel smiled.

"But if I recall, your medallion doesn't have any writing." Elizabeth thought back to her examination of the artifact at dinner.

"No, there is not." Manuel gave a half smile to the others.

"You mentioned magic," Elizabeth said.

"Yes, magical powers."

"Magic to do what?" Jack asked.

"Whatever is necessary." Manuel's voice was cold.

Manuel's description of the medallions left the wheel room silent as everyone wondered what he meant by his last comment.

Finally, Manuel burst out laughing. "You don't believe that, do you? It's just an old myth. Please, magic in a medallion? How absurd. I got you, no?"

Everyone responded with controlled laughter. No one besides Manuel had ever heard of such a myth.

"That one does look better than the other medallion," Shawn said.

Manuel's smile faded immediately, and his face turned deadly serious. "There is another one?"

Shawn looked confused. "Yeah, I thought Jack told you."

"No, he did not." Manuel stared at Jack. "Why was this kept from me?"

"Actually there were six medallions, but four of them were trashed, and the other, well, ah, Jack . . ." Shawn stuttered nervously and looked toward his boss.

Elizabeth sensed that something was wrong as she watched Manuel's pleasant expression change to one of anger.

"Manuel, please understand that we brought up so much stuff, some good, some not so good," Jack began. "I have been studying this kind of thing for years, and I know good pieces from bad. That other medallion was worthless. It had these crazy symbols on each side that we couldn't make out, like some ancient language, but it wasn't in our computers, and you did say we were the best. I figured that the other medallion was junk, so I gave you the better of the two." Jack looked around for help, saw none, and continued. "Besides, Manuel, you want the best for your family and, believe me, this medallion is so much better than the other."

Manuel's expression never changed. "Did this worthless medallion have a blue stone in it?"

"Yes," Jack said. "As a matter of fact, it did."

"And you mentioned crazy markings?" Manuel's eyes narrowed.

Jack stammered, "Yeah, but we couldn't find them in our computer."

Manuel looked at his bodyguards, but they did not react. The multibillionaire glared at Jack, who glanced at Elizabeth and Shawn, confused at the sudden turn of events.

"And what did you do with this supposedly worthless medallion?" Manuel demanded.

Jack shrugged. "I sent it to my nephew. Why?"

EIGHT

A PACKAGE ARRIVES

THE UPS DRIVER JUMPED down from his truck. The package he carried wasn't very big. He placed it on the doorstep, rang the doorbell, and walked back to his truck.

Tommy's dad opened the door, cursing at the driver for bothering him, but the other man didn't hear him as he drove off in the brown truck.

Unshaven and wearing the same clothes he wore the night before, Eric Reed picked up the package. He glanced at the return address in the corner of the envelope and cringed; it was from his brother.

Eric walked into the house and slammed the door behind him. His wife's eyes opened wide as she sat on the couch, trying to blend in with the fabric so Eric wouldn't notice her. He headed to Tommy's room.

He burst through the door and kicked the bed where Tommy slept. Tommy jolted up, surprised at the unannounced wake-up call.

"What?" Tommy squinted at the intrusive light.

"Here is a thing from your Uncle Jack ... again." Eric threw the package onto the bed.

Tommy's eyes burst open. He didn't want to seem too ecstatic so as not to upset his dad, so he nonchalantly grabbed the manila envelope and tossed it onto his desk.

"I'll open it later." He fell back into bed.

Eric squinted one eye at his son and picked his teeth with his tongue before suddenly screaming at Tommy.

"You know, your Uncle Jack isn't that special of a guy! He left me here to go running around the world, and that's all anyone can ever talk about. When Mom died, your grandma, he didn't even bother to show up to the funeral! 'Mr. Globetrotter' is a phony who should be in prison!"

"Dad, he did show up at Grandma's funeral," Tommy said. "Remember, he spoke at the cemetery?"

Tommy's dad stared hard at his son. "Are you saying I'm a liar?"

Tommy realized his mistake. "No, sir."

"Good. You just watch yourself. I don't want to see you end up like my selfish brother. He only cares about himself and that precious crew of his. Do you understand me?"

Tommy nodded, afraid to speak.

"Good!" his dad said again. He walked out, slamming the door behind him.

Tommy heard his dad mumbling to himself as he descended the steps. "Should be me out there, not here having to deal with all of this. But he stepped over me and never bothered to ask if I wanted to go ... rotten son of a ..."

When he heard his dad clear the steps, Tommy leapt from the bed and tore open the package like a kid at Christmas. A hand-sized medallion with a tarnished blue stone fell onto the floor. Tommy reached inside the envelope and grabbed the handwritten note. "Found something from the bottom of the sea. Uncle Jack."

Tommy couldn't believe it. He stared at the newfound treasure and studied every detail of the medallion. *The strange markings must mean something*, Tommy thought, *but they sure were weird looking*. And the blue stone needed to be cleaned. He reached for his cellphone and pushed a number. Tommy waited a minute for Chris to pick up.

"Chris ... Tommy, yeah I'm good. Hey, can you meet me at the clubhouse ... because my Uncle Jack just sent me something and I want the Club to see it ... great ... I'll see you in half an hour."

Tommy closed the phone and turned his attention back to the medallion. It felt smooth in his hands as he rubbed his index finger over the markings and the blue stone.

Rough, he thought, holding the medallion closer to his eyes to get a better look at the markings. They were like nothing he had ever seen.

He couldn't remember ever being this excited, except maybe the last time his uncle sent him something. Smiling from ear to ear, Tommy put the medallion on his desk. Feeling newly energized, he began to get dressed.

NINE

A REAL TREASURE FIND

CHRIS SWIPED HIS KEY card and entered the Treasure Hunters clubhouse. He found Tommy sitting at the meeting table. Chris's eyes went right to the medallion.

"That's it?" Chris was a little disappointed.

Tommy seemed confused. "What do you mean, 'that's it'? Come on and look at it. My Uncle Jack sent it to me from the bottom of the Caribbean Sea."

Chris picked up the old relic and looked at it quizzically.

"What are these markings?"

"Not sure," Tommy said. "They are obviously another language, but not one I've ever seen."

"And the blue stone?" Chris placed his finger on it. "What is this?"

Tommy shrugged. "I don't know. A stone. What do I look like, a geologist?"

"No, but shouldn't we know all this stuff before we start calling it a treasure?"

"The point is that my Uncle Jack—a real treasure hunter, mind you—sent it to me for the Club, and I would appreciate it if you would get a little more excited."

Chris smiled weakly. "Yippee."

Shannon and Jackson walked in a minute later.

"Great, you guys are here," Chris said. "Look at the new treasure."

Shannon grabbed the medallion first, to the obvious disappointment of Jackson. She studied the artifact very closely. "What are these markings?"

"Same thing we were wondering," Tommy said.

"Can I see it?" Jackson asked.

"In a minute."

"You always say that and ..." Jackson hesitated as Shannon glared at him. "Why don't you take your time," he said, joining the others at the table.

"I've never seen anything like this before," Shannon said, "and this stone doesn't look like a polished gem."

"Then what is it?" Chris asked.

"Feels like a really rough rock."

"Why put a rock in a medallion?" Tommy asked.

"Don't know. Maybe like the markings that we don't recognize, the stone was considered a jewel long ago. Someone did take the time to put it into a medallion. Could be this culture believed that a colored stone held great value or something."

"May I see it now?" Jackson asked politely. Shannon handed it to him and sat down.

"I think I agree with Shannon," Jackson said.

"Big surprise," she said.

"I'm serious. We don't know what these people took for value. And maybe putting the stone in a gold medallion helped a king or something."

"So what's our next move?" Tommy asked.

"I think we go to the library and start researching the markings to see what we can learn about that stone," Shannon said.

"Why not use the computer here?" Chris asked. "I hate riding my bike that far."

"Our Internet connection is too slow. All of us need to work on this," Shannon said.

"Then let's go." Tommy put the medallion in his backpack.

"What are you doing?" Shannon asked.

"What?"

"You're putting the medallion in your backpack?" Jackson stared at him.

"What's the problem?"

"The problem is that you could lose it!" Chris chimed in.

"I will not!" Tommy was defensive.

"Like the original 1913 buffalo coins?" Shannon said.

Leave it to Shannon, Tommy thought, to remember the time just after he had formed the Treasure Hunters Club when his Uncle Jack sent him a set of the first printed 1913 buffalo coins by James Earle Fraser. Tommy promptly lost the set of coins within an hour of receiving them. However, with the help of Shannon and Jackson, they found them in the field behind the clubhouse. Tommy still kept a few of the coins in his backpack.

"I guess you're right," Tommy said. "I'll put it in the safe."

"Wait." Jackson took out his cellphone and snapped several pictures of the medallion. "There." He put his phone back in his pocket. "Now we won't have go on memory."

"I could just bring it," Tommy said.

In unison the Club yelled, "No!"

"Okay, okay."

After the coin incident, the Club created a custom-built safe in the bathroom underneath the toilet. The safe had an automatic camera that took still shots of whoever opened the door.

Tommy moved the toilet aside and worked the combination. He heard the lock click and turned the handle. The door opened, and Tommy heard the small snap of the camera. He smiled and placed the medallion in the safe, then closed the door. Spinning the knob on the safe, he moved the toilet into its original spot and walked back to the group.

"Is that the first time we've actually used that safe?" Jackson asked.

"For something this big," Shannon said.

"All right then," Tommy said, "let's go."

The Treasure Hunters Club walked out of their clubhouse, got on their bikes, and started the trip to the downtown library.

Inside the safe, the medallion began to glow brightly. The mysterious beam lit up the entire bathroom in a clear, brilliant blue color.

* * *

Juan rummaged through papers and found a black ledger book. He opened it and found a receipt from UPS.

"Got it," Juan said as he and Conrado walked back to the cabin where Manuel sat waiting. Jack and Elizabeth struggled to free their hands from the nylon ropes binding them. When Manuel found out what Jack had done with the other medallion, he flew into a rage.

Manuel commanded Juan and Conrado to work Jack over for some information about Tommy, but Jack never caved, despite the assault.

"I don't get it. What's so special about that other medallion?" Jack asked.

"I told you about the ultimate power that both medallions bring when they are put together. Those crazy symbols, as you have said, are the key to the power that is rightfully mine."

Jack laughed through the pain racing through his body. "You believe that? Manuel, those kinds of stories are everywhere around this area. You said yourself, it is a myth. Come on, haven't you ever heard of fishing stories? I once caught a fish 'this big,' kind of thing. I would think that a man of your intelligence wouldn't fall for something so stupid."

Manuel slapped Jack across the face and grabbed his blood-stained shirt. "Some myths are true, Jack. Just like your blue diamond mine that made you so famous!" He slapped Jack again and walked away.

"*El Jefe*," Juan began as he entered the wheel room, "we found this receipt."

"Good." Manuel smiled at Jack. "Nice of UPS to put the tracking number on the receipt."

Manuel pulled out his cellphone and began punching numbers. It took only a few seconds for him to connect to the Internet and pull up the UPS website. Three minutes later, he had Tommy Reed's address.

"I love modern technology." Manuel turned off his phone and placed it in his side pocket. "Makes things move much faster, don't you think, Jack?"

Jack lifted his beaten face and tried to say something clever, but couldn't. The situation now seemed beyond his control, and words couldn't match the moment.

"We need to call our friends and make sure they can have a team in the air within the next hour," Manuel said to Juan, who began taking notes. "We will need to know when they have made contact and when the medallion is in their possession."

"*El Jefe*," Conrado said, "we could take the plane ourselves and handle this."

"No." Manuel shook his head. "I need you to take care of other things for me." He turned to Jack and Elizabeth. "I am so sorry it has to end this way, Jack. You are very good at what you do, but alas, everyone must someday meet his Maker. And Elizabeth, ahh, another time, another place, we might have been together. But unfortunately it will never be." He kissed her forehead as she turned her head away, her every muscle hurting.

Manuel looked at Juan and Conrado. "I want this operation done quickly. Make the calls now and let me know when it is done."

"What would you like us to do with them?" Juan asked.

Manuel smiled. "Take them out as far as you can and feed them to the fishes."

"And the boat?"

"We'll keep that as payment for not completing the job. Okay with you, Jack?"

Jack spit on the white tile floor. "Sure Manuel, whatever."

"I know." Manuel left the cabin.

"What's going to happen now?" Elizabeth asked Jack.

"I think we're going to have to become really good swimmers."

They both heard the powerful engines of the *Hanoj* roar as it started moving out to sea.

TEN

THE LIBRARY

THE LIBRARY WAS LOCATED a few miles from
Tommy's house. The Club weaved and raced through the
streets to arrive in only forty minutes.

During the summer, the library had undergone a
facelift, and a new coffee shop had been added as well as an
expanded audiovisual room.

The Club members swept through the coffee shop.
They waved to Alice, the manager, as if they were regulars in
a bar.

Tommy pointed to the reference section. The club
found a large table and dumped their backpacks on top of it,
then proceeded to search through the volumes of books.

"I guess we should check under M," Chris said.

"What about L for lost treasure?"

"Very funny, Tommy," Shannon said.

"I'm going to the computers. This book stuff is
going to take too long." Jackson opened his cellphone and
emailed the picture of the medallion to the others.

"Check your email if you need the picture." He
walked away.

Jackson made his way to the computer section of
the library. Thirty computers lined the walls of the spacious

room. Jackson signed in at the main desk and sat at the first available computer. He moved the mouse quickly and clicked his way to the Internet.

Tommy, Chris, and Shannon pored over books about lost treasure and amazing artifacts.

One book that caught Shannon's eyes was called *Ancient Hoaxes*. She flipped through the pages and read several stories, but found nothing of real interest until she reached the last section.

The chapter was titled "Magical Artifacts," and the first picture staring her in the face was of Tommy's medallion.

She turned the open book toward Chris and Tommy. "This look familiar."

Both boys looked up from their books at the same time and stared at the picture. There was the same medallion with its crazy symbols and unique blue stone.

"What does it say?" Tommy asked.

Shannon pulled the book back and began reading aloud.

"'According to legend, a gypsy woman was entrusted to protect this particular medallion from the Dorcha, who were followers of dark magic, and she died mysteriously. No one has ever found the medallion or has any idea of its whereabouts.' It also says that 'anyone who has possession of the medallion can tap into its magical powers.'" She looked up at Tommy. "That doesn't sound too bad."

Tommy nodded. "Just keep reading."

"Sorry. 'After many years of research and study, it was found that gypsies used the medallions to frighten people through magic. However, gypsies did not have the ability to use magic in that way.' Your medallion, by the way, was lost during a storm—wait, check that, a hurricane—in the early 1700s. The markings are an ancient language that no one has deciphered, though it is possibly from an extinct Indian tribe, but 'most analysts agree the markings mean nothing.'"

"How can that be?" Tommy said, surprised.

"Someone could have engraved them as their own special cipher or something," Shannon said.

"Maybe your uncle just wanted to send you a gift and thought it looked cool," Chris added.

Tommy's eyes dropped. "Man, I thought we finally had found a really important artifact."

"Oh, Tommy," Shannon said. "This is just a starting point. We have more research to do."

"Or," Tommy suggested, "we might as well take it to the exhibits at the Civic Center."

"You love that exhibit," Chris said, amazed.

"I do, but I really thought this might be the Club's first treasure."

"Actually, you could probably sell the medallion to Mr. Thornberry, the director of the exhibit. He's always looking for new stuff," Chris said.

Shannon shook her head. "Wait until we learn more about the medallion, Tommy. Someone thought it was important three hundred years ago."

His friends' comments did little to help Tommy's mood. The rush he felt when he received the medallion had already dissolved, and he closed the book he was reading and got up from the table. "I'm going to get a drink."

"All right." Chris returned his eyes to the book he had been reading.

"Tommy," Shannon said, "are you going to be okay?"

Tommy nodded and walked away.

"Nice sensitivity." Shannon glared at Chris.

"What? That?" Chris looked surprised. "He'll be fine. I say we head to the Mythological Artifacts Exhibit and sell it."

"Always money with you." Shannon shook her head.

"What good is it to be a treasure hunter if you are always poor?"

"Whatever." Shannon waved her hand dismissively.

Jackson came down the hallway carrying four sheets of paper.

"I found it," he said, handing the papers to Shannon.

"Yeah." She leafed through the black and white pictures identical to those in the book. "We've already read about it."

"No way," Jackson said in surprise.

Both Shannon and Chris nodded.

"Then you know about the gypsies?"

"Yes."

"And the dark magic?"

"Yes."

"And the special magic put into the medallion that we have?"

"Yes."

"And the *second* medallion?"

Caught off guard, neither answered him right away.

"What second medallion?" Shannon finally asked.

"You mean I found out something the great Shannon McDougal did not?"

"Just tell us," Shannon said firmly.

"Let me enjoy this for a second." A satisfied grin spread across Jackson's face.

Losing her patience, Shannon rose from her seat. "You've got two seconds before I beat it out of you."

Jackson realized his moment was over. "According to what I found, the gypsies were asked by a group called the Leois to put the power of magic into two medallions."

"We only read about one," Shannon said.

"What kind of magic?" Chris asked.

"The power of light or dark."

"Power of light or dark?" Shannon asked.

"Yeah." Jackson picked up the papers and started to read. "The Leois were afraid the Dorcha—"

"Followers of the dark magic," Shannon interrupted.

"Yeah," Jackson said. "The Leois believed that combining both sides of magic would create some kind of super power that no one group should control. So they had the gypsies separate them."

"And?" Chris stood up, an interested expression on his face.

"You know one medallion has a blue stone and the other a red," Jackson said.

"Red?" Chris said.

"It has the dark magic inside it. You know—evil."

"So if it's separated, what's the big deal?" Shannon asked.

"If you do this," Jackson said, clasping his hands together, "and put the two medallions together . . ."

Shannon and Chris remained silent and stared at Jackson. "Yeah?" they said in unison.

"Followers of the Leois and Dorcha believed you would have the ultimate power for good and evil," Jackson finished.

"So we don't have the other medallion, which makes ours worthless?" Shannon asked.

"Not necessarily. From what I read on the Internet, a single medallion was thought to have some magical properties. Just not as much power as if you had the two, but I didn't find out what kind or how to use it."

"The book, *Ancient Hoaxes*, said any person in possession of the medallion would be able to use its magic," Shannon said.

Tommy walked back to the table carrying a can of soda.

"Hey, Jackson. Find anything?"

"I'll say," Shannon said, and handed the papers to Tommy.

"What are these?" Tommy put down the can.

"Just read them and look at the picture."

Tommy started to read, but couldn't believe his eyes. He stopped and stared at the group. He felt a wave of energy flow through him. "This is unbelievable."

"Do you believe what it says about the magic is true?" Jackson asked.

Tommy shrugged. "Let's keep working to find out."

✣　　✣　　✣

The Gulf Stream jet landed and taxied to an empty hangar in a deserted part of the small airport.

Two men emerged from the plane. Both were powerfully built; the man with brown hair was named Gavin, and the one with darker hair was named Dillon.

A black Mercedes pulled up. A driver stepped out and handed Dillon the keys.

"Here's the address." The driver handed a slip of paper to Dillon.

"Photo?" Gavin asked.

"One in the car."

"All right." Dillon motioned for Gavin to get inside. They sped toward the exit and onto the highway.

ELEVEN

FISH FOOD

WATER SPLASHED THE SIDE of *Hanoj* as the boat sped out to sea. Juan piloted while Conrado guarded the prisoners.

Jack started to wiggle his hands free, feeling the rope loosen even as it burned deeper into his wrists with every turn. Jack caught Elizabeth's attention and motioned for her to try to free her own hands, but she returned a defeated look that only fueled Jack's resolve.

"Conrado, where is my crew?" Jack asked.

"Manuel took care of them."

"What do you mean by that?"

"Does it matter? You can't do anything about it now anyway."

Jack heard the motors stop and the boat began pitching against the gentle waves.

Juan walked over to Jack and Elizabeth. He looked at both of them and smiled, shaking his head. "You know we hate to do this."

"That's funny, because I thought you guys liked this kind of stuff," Jack said.

"It was nice of Mr. Ernesto to allow you to die with a friend, don't you think?" Juan smiled broadly. "Bind them."

Conrado pulled out two sets of ankle weights and showed them to Jack and Elizabeth.

"Who's first?"

"The great treasure hunter," Juan said to his partner. "I'll cover you." He removed a .38 caliber pistol from his coat.

Conrado bent down and wrapped the weights around Jack's ankles. Jack judged them to be about fifteen to twenty pounds. Conrado then turned his attention to Elizabeth, who sat quietly, resigned to her impending doom.

"Elizabeth?" Jack said.

She looked at him with sorrowful eyes.

"Don't give up yet."

"Why?"

"Because," Jack yelled, swinging his right arm free and slapping the gun from Juan's hand. The pistol slid across the floor.

Jack freed himself and picked up a chair. He swung it into Juan's chest, shattering the chair to pieces and knocking Juan to the ground.

Conrado lunged at Jack and planted a foot into his back. The treasure hunter fell forward, but bounced up again quickly and landed a right cross to Conrado's jaw, dropping the large man. Jack swung around and caught Juan in the midsection with a powerful kick. Both bodyguards rolled around on the ground in pain.

Jack ran to Elizabeth and untied her hands just as Conrado and Juan regained their footing. They all saw the gun lying on the floor and dove for it. Bodies smashed against one another as the gun slipped out of everyone's reach.

Juan grabbed Jack and took a swing at his face. Jack ducked out of the way, and Juan's fist connected with Conrado's nose instead, knocking the big man back. Conrado's eyes closed as he slumped to the ground.

Juan, who still held Jack by the shirt, slammed him several times against the wall. Jack's body started to fall limp in Juan's large paws.

The click of a cocking gun caused Juan to stop.

Elizabeth held the .38 revolver, seeming quite comfortable with its weight in her hands. Her arms were steady as she pointed it at Juan and gave him a steely-eyed stare.

"Let him go."

"You wouldn't dare." Juan smirked.

Elizabeth moved the gun slightly and fired. The bullet whizzed past Juan's head and hit the console.

"Try me," she said.

Conrado attempted to stand, but stumbled and fell against the wheelhouse door.

"Put Jack down, Juan, and pick up Conrado. He needs your help," Elizabeth said.

Juan reluctantly let go of Jack, who shook his head, straightened his shirt, and nodded at the large Spaniard.

"What's next?" Jack asked Elizabeth.

"Time to see if these boys can swim."

"You are not going to throw us in the water?" Juan's voice was fearful

"Of course not," Elizabeth said.

"Good." Juan steadied Conrado.

"Both of you are going to jump in." Elizabeth smiled.

Jack grabbed the used rope and wrapped it around Juan and Conrado. He pulled them closer to the edge of the boat.

"Any last words?" Jack asked.

"We are not going to jump," Juan said defiantly.

"No problem." Jack pushed the two bodyguards off the side and into the water. He turned to Elizabeth with a wink. "Let's go."

Jack pulled the cord on the compressed gas cartridge of a yellow raft and tossed it over the side, watching it inflate.

"Rowing thirty-five miles will keep them busy," he said.

Jack stood at the console and turned the key. The engines roared as he pushed the gas and headed back to Port Royal Harbor.

"We need to get ahold of Tommy before Manuel does," Jack said.

"Can we call from here?"

"No. You shot the radio, Liz. And Juan and Conrado destroyed our cellphones."

"We'll call when we reach port." Elizabeth paused. "Do you think he already got to Tommy?"

"I hope not," Jack said as he revved the motor for more speed.

TWELVE

SURPRISE GUESTS

TOMMY WATCHED HIS FRIENDS ride away as he
stood in the driveway, dreading the next moments. He knew
his father probably spent all day stewing about his life while
Tommy's mother worked quietly around the house trying
not to upset anyone or anything.

Tommy thought for a moment about continuing to
ride, but he didn't. Instead he parked his bike, took a deep
breath, and walked in the front door.

"Where have you been?" his father snapped.

"The library." Tommy placed his backpack on a
wooden bench.

"What for?"

"Just looking up stuff."

"With those friends of yours?"

Tommy's dad never liked anyone, and especially
resented Tommy's friends. Not that he had ever gotten to
know them or even their names, Tommy thought. However,
Tommy's dad constantly complained that they were spoiled,
misbehaving brats. Once Tommy tried to argue, got a swift
slap, and never spoke about it again.

"Yeah, Dad. What's for dinner?" he asked, trying
to change the subject.

"Your mother made something," Eric waved a dismissive hand toward the kitchen.

"Hey, Mom, what are we eating?"

"Rigatoni with garlic bread."

"Great." Tommy tried to sound excited.

Dinner at the Reed house used to be fun. Tommy's parents once got along, and told funny stories, but as Tommy grew older, times changed. After his father lost his job, he drifted into a deep depression while his mother retreated inside herself. A cold silence laced its way through the house and into every meal.

Tommy sat at the square table with his mom at one end near the stove and his dad at the other. The rigatoni looked great, and Tommy dug into the bowl. Pasta was one of his favorite meals, but since he was starving almost anything would have tasted good.

Tommy's dad ate a few bites of rigatoni, slammed back a beer, and got up without finishing his meal. Grumbling beneath his breath, he walked into the family room and turned on the television.

"I saw you got a package from your Uncle Jack," Tommy's mom whispered.

"Yeah." Tommy took care not to raise his voice too loud.

"What was it?"

"Just some fake artifact Uncle Jack says he found at the bottom of the Caribbean Sea."

"Must be nice there." His mom gazed out the window.

"Not as fun as here." Tommy smiled, trying to cheer up his mom.

She looked at him and smiled the way mothers smile at their sons. "I guess not," she said. "Are you finished?"

"Yeah, thanks."

Tommy's mom grabbed his plate, then placed it on hers and walked to the sink to wash them.

A moment later, both turned their heads at the sound of the doorbell.

Eric answered the door with his usual rudeness.

"What do you want?" he yelled.

Two men wearing suits and sunglasses smiled back at him. One flashed his badge so quickly that Tommy's dad didn't really think he saw anything.

"Hello, is this the Reed residence?" the brown-haired man asked.

"Who wants to know?"

"I am Agent Gavin with the FBI and this is Agent Dillon."

"Yeah, so?"

"Are you the father of one Thomas Reed?" Dillon asked.

"Is he in trouble?"

Both men laughed. "No, not at all. We just have some questions to ask him."

Tommy's dad shook his head. "Boy's in trouble with the government now. Tommy, come here, these men want to talk with you."

Tommy's cellphone rang, but he made no attempt to pick it up.

"Pick it up, will ya!" Tommy's dad yelled.

Tommy walked through the family room and saw the two men dressed in black. Just before he reached the doorway, he grabbed his phone and opened it.

"Hello," Tommy said.

"Tommy?" The voice sounded hurried.

"Yes."

"It's Uncle Jack."

Tommy's eyes lit up. "Hey, I was just—"

His uncle quickly cut him off. "No time for talk, Tommy. Did you get the medallion I sent you?"

"Yes."

"Have you told anyone about it?"

"Just the Club."

"Tommy, you must listen carefully to what I'm about to say. Don't freak out or anything. I need you to be treasure-hunter-cool, okay?"

"Okay."

"You are in great danger because of that medallion."

Tommy heard the words "great danger" and froze, his eyes fixed on the men talking to his dad at the front door.

"So what do I do?" Tommy whispered.

"Hide the medallion," Jack said. "Guard it with your life. If anyone comes looking for it, make up some story, but do not let it go."

"All right," Tommy said. "I think some people are here now."

Jack breathed deeply into the phone. "Say nothing. I'm on my way. Be safe."

Tommy closed the phone slowly. As he looked at his father and the two men, he could feel his heart racing.

"Let's go, boy, these men are busy," his dad yelled.

Tommy stuffed the phone in his pocket and walked to the front door.

"Hi," Tommy said. He managed to smile.

"Thomas Reed, I am Agent Gavin and this is Agent Dillon. We are with the FBI." One of the men flashed his badge quicker than the eye could see.

"You can call me Tommy. Am I in trouble or something?"

"No, Tommy, you're not," Agent Gavin said. "We just need you to answer a few questions for us."

"Okay."

"About your Uncle Jack," Gavin emphasized.

"Now *he* should be arrested," Tommy's dad blurted out.

Tommy stared at his dad in anger, and then remembered what his uncle said about treasure-hunter-cool. "Sure, I can answer."

"When was the last time you saw your uncle?"

"About a year ago."

"When was the last time you spoke with him?" Dillon joined the conversation.

"I haven't," Tommy said. "I got an email from him a week ago. He said he was in the Caribbean doing an excavation."

"Has he sent you any packages recently?" Gavin asked.

Without missing a beat, Tommy said, "Yes, would you like to see?"

Gavin gave Dillon a nod of confidence.

"Definitely."

"It's in my book bag." Tommy started rifling through the notebooks and folders. He unzipped a pocket where he kept some of the buffalo coins Jack had sent him years before.

"Here." Tommy held the four coins in the palm of his hand. "Pretty cool, huh? These are actually originals printed in 1913."

"Was that what that UPS guy dropped off the other day?" Eric turned to the agents. "Woke me up from my nap."

"Right," Tommy said, relieved. "The UPS package. That's it."

Gavin and Dillon's surprised expression was not lost on Tommy, who plowed ahead.

"If these are stolen, you can have them back. I don't want to get Uncle Jack or myself in any trouble."

Both men looked at the coins, stunned.

"No," Gavin said, "that isn't what we are looking for."

"Then what?" Tommy asked. "I mean, if I know what it is maybe I could help."

"A medallion," Dillon said.

Tommy's insides jumped at the word, but outwardly he remained calm. "Sorry, sirs, but my Uncle Jack has never sent me anything like that."

Gavin nodded. "Well, then, thank you for your time. We are going to check out some other leads around town."

"Okay." Tommy felt sweat forming on his palms.

"We'll check back in a couple of days," Gavin added, "in case the medallion should arrive."

"If it does I'll hold it for you." Tommy smiled.

"Goodbye," Gavin said as Dillon waved and followed him to the car.

Tommy shut the door and breathed a sigh of relief. His dad walked to the couch, grabbed the remote, and resumed watching television.

Tommy peered through the drapes as the two men got in their car and drove away. Stepping back from the window, Tommy saw that his hands were shaking and prayed that the two men hadn't noticed.

"I told you my brother was no good," Eric said.

Tommy looked at his dad before returning to the window. His hands wouldn't stop shaking, and he really wished they would.

THIRTEEN

FLEEING

TOMMY COULDN'T GET TO the clubhouse fast
enough. He pushed a button on his cellphone to call Chris
and waited for him to answer.

"Hello?"

"Chris, it's Tommy."

"Hey, long time no see."

"Can you come over?"

"It's getting late," Chris said. "We just finished
dinner."

"I know, but something has happened and it's about
the medallion."

"What about it?"

"I can't tell you over the phone. Just come over and
call Shannon and Jackson too."

"You're starting to sound weird," Chris said. "Are
you in some kind of danger?"

"Just get everybody and come over." Tommy ended
the call and closed his phone.

Once inside the clubhouse, Tommy walked toward
the small safe and stopped. What if the medallion really
was magical? Could he handle that truth? He wondered why
his Uncle Jack would have sent something that would get
him in trouble. Besides, what would he do with a magical
medallion anyway?

Many questions, Tommy thought, *and no answers.*
Tommy stepped into the bathroom and moved the toilet.
He pressed several numbers on the keypad and waited to
hear the lock click open. When it did, he grabbed the
medallion and examined it quizzically. The blue stone in the
middle looked so small that he wondered if something that
size could even possess magic. And were those markings a
magical saying from long ago? Tommy decided the
medallion didn't seem all that magical; in fact, it looked
rather ordinary.

He turned it over in his hands and stared closely at
the markings. Tommy figured Uncle Jack must know what
they mean. *But why wouldn't he tell him over the phone? He knew his
uncle wouldn't purposely put him in danger.*

A knock on the door startled Tommy and he
dropped the medallion. As he picked it up off the floor,
Tommy looked at the video security monitors and saw the
FBI agents standing outside with his dad.

He stuffed the medallion into his pocket, closed the
safe, and pushed the toilet back into place.

Another knock and Tommy's mind started to race.
He had to get out of the clubhouse.

Tommy moved the sink and stared at the man-sized
hole leading to the underground tunnel the group had dug.
He had been against building it because he could never
imagine any kind of emergency that would require slipping
out of the clubhouse unseen. Now he silently thanked the
others for insisting on an escape route.

Tommy slipped easily into the tunnel. He pulled the sink back into place behind him and started the long crawl. The group originally wanted to build tunnels large enough for standing, but without any money they were happy to have a crawl space instead.

The tunnel stretched one hundred yards and ended at the middle of the old airfield behind Tommy's house.

When he reached the end, Tommy lifted the plank covering the tunnel, stepped into the twilight, and found himself surrounded by shabby trees, overgrown brush, and bushes. He slid the board over the hole and looked off into the distance. He could see the outlines of his father and the two agents against the fading sunlight. As he stared down the road leading to his house, he could just make out the shapes of three familiar bike riders. Tommy sprinted through the tall weeds, hoping to cut off Chris and the others before they reached the clubhouse.

☆   ☆   ☆

"I heard him come out here," Tommy's dad said, slamming his fist on the door. "He's always out here."

"That's all right," Gavin said, holding his temper.

"You guys came back awfully fast." Eric knocked again.

"We had some questions we forgot to ask Tommy. Now that we know he spends a lot of time here, we'll know where to find him. Thanks."

Gavin and Dillon walked back to their car. Gavin pulled out his cellphone and punched a button. Instantly, Manuel was on the phone.

"Yes, sir, we've made contact." Gavin paused, listening to the voice on the other line. "No, we don't have the medallion yet, but we are confident that we will in the next couple of days." Gavin paused again. "We know, no collateral damage, yes sir ... okay. Goodbye." Gavin closed his phone and put it in his jacket pocket.

"What did he say?" Dillon asked.

"He said to take care of this quickly."

*   *   *

Tommy came through the field and looked down the road. He saw the silhouettes of his three friends riding their bikes toward his house. He ran at them as fast as he could.

"Is that Tommy?" Shannon asked.

"Why is he running?" Jackson wondered out loud.

Tommy waved his arms frantically. "Hide," he yelled. "Hide."

When Tommy reached the bikers, it took him a minute to catch his breath.

"What is with you?" Chris looked at him in concern.

"My ..." Tommy took a deep breath. "My Uncle Jack called and ..." Tommy inhaled again. "He said that the medallion has put me in danger. Then these two FBI guys show up at the house FBI and ..."

"Wait," Shannon interrupted, "the FBI?"

Tommy glanced over his shoulder and saw the black Mercedes pulling out of his driveway.

"In here!" he screamed, pushing Shannon and her bike into the abandoned airfield as Chris and Jackson followed.

"Get down," Tommy said, lying on top of Shannon.

"From what? And get off me!" She pushed him onto his side.

"Just shh."

Though it seemed like hours, the car sped past the Treasure Hunters Club only a minute after they had ducked into the field. Tommy got up, as did the others. They brushed the dirt and leaves off their clothes and walked toward the street, each of them staring hard at Tommy.

Tommy didn't notice their looks. "My Uncle Jack called and told me to hide the medallion," he said. "I don't think those are FBI guys, but they kept asking if Uncle Jack has ever sent me any packages."

"What did you tell them?" Jackson asked.

"Why do you have to hide the medallion?" Shannon wondered aloud.

"One thing at a time," Tommy said. "I told the two guys he had sent me stuff and I showed them the old buffalo coins."

"The buffalo coins?" Chris looked surprised.

"Yeah." Tommy looked over his shoulder to see if anyone was coming.

"Then what?" Jackson said.

"So they left and I went to the clubhouse and called Chris."

"Then why rush to meet all of us out here?" Shannon asked.

"Because after I talked to Chris those FBI guys came back and went to the clubhouse pounding on the door."

"How'd you get out?" Jackson asked.

"The escape tunnel."

Jackson smiled. The tunnel had been his idea. "You mean you actually used it?"

"Do you have the medallion?" Shannon asked.

"Yes."

"So what are you going to do?" Jackson asked.

"Chris, can I stay at your house tonight? Tell your parents we have a big project due tomorrow at school."

"I'm sure it will be okay," Chris said.

"What about tomorrow?" Jackson asked.

"My Uncle Jack said he was on his way. So I will go to school as usual."

"Why?" Shannon wondered.

"It'll be the safest place until my uncle arrives."

That night, Tommy pulled the covers over his shoulders and tried to close his eyes. His mom said it was all right for him to stay at Chris's house. She didn't bother to tell Tommy's dad, because she knew it would be easier for her son that way.

"Tommy?" Chris called from across the room.

"What?"

"Is it really magical? The medallion, I mean?"

Tommy pulled the medallion out from under his pillow and examined it once more.

"Doesn't seem like it."

"I figured." Chris sounded disappointed.

"Me too."

All this trouble, Tommy thought, *and the medallion probably didn't even have any magic. Nice piece of treasure, Uncle Jack.*

FOURTEEN

THE SAFEST PLACE

TOMMY STEPPED OFF THE bus at Kennedy Middle School and scanned the parking lot in search of the black Mercedes, but he found nothing. Tommy could sense the FBI guys out there somewhere. Chris, on the other hand, walked in front of Tommy without a care in the world.

A hand touched Tommy's shoulder and he jumped, dropping his backpack. It was Jackson.

"Are you all right?" his friend asked.

"Yeah, just a little nervous." Tommy smiled and shouldered his pack.

"How did it go last night? Did you sleep?"

"Not much."

A bell rang, signaling for the students to get to their first-period class.

"I'll see you at lunch," Jackson said.

"Let's get to Mr. Sims's class." Chris turned to go, but stopped when he saw the look on Tommy's face.

"It will be safe in here," he said. "Your Uncle Jack will be here soon, and no one is going to get you in school."

"What about Zach?"

Chris thought for a moment. "Good point, but at least we know Shannon can take Zach. Let's go."

Tommy reluctantly agreed, and the two friends walked into the middle school, hoping to have an ordinary day.

Tommy moved through the school day as he normally did. By this late in the school year, walking between classes had become so routine that he could probably get to each one with his eyes closed.

However, Tommy still couldn't help feeling nervous. Like in art class, when he fell out of his chair after the class phone rang. This drew much laughter from everyone, including himself.

As he walked the hallways, Tommy kept an eye out for Agents Gavin and Dillon. At one point he thought he saw them, and dove into the bathroom only to discover the two men were janitors.

It was during this bathroom hideaway that Tommy ran into an even bigger problem—his old friend, Zach Butler.

"Hey there, Tommy boy."

Tommy turned around, fixing his eyes on the big eighth grader standing before him.

"Oh, hi, Zach," Tommy said, at the same time wondering whether Zach had grown even bigger since yesterday.

Zach lumbered toward Tommy. "I think we have some unfinished business to take care of."

"Too bad I can't stay." Tommy dove to the ground, did a summersault, and fell into the hallway before sprinting away. As he ran, Tommy thought he heard Zach mention something about lunchtime, but he was gone so quickly he couldn't be sure.

❊   ❊   ❊

Jackson and Chris met up with Tommy just outside the cafeteria doors with a bully update.

"Coast is clear," Jackson said. "Zach got in a fight last period."

"He's got In-School Suspension for the rest of the day," Chris said.

For the first time all day, Tommy felt some relief. He put his hands in his pockets and felt the medallion. *All this for a piece of junk that doesn't have any magic,* Tommy thought again, shaking his head in disgust.

After getting their lunches, the group sat at a table near the exit. Tommy positioned himself with his back to the other students so he could see who walked in and out of the lunchroom.

Tommy was choking down several bites of the school's pizza when suddenly he felt a massive hand on his shoulder. He wanted to turn, but the strength of the hand forced him to remain in place.

"Thought I'd forgotten about you?" the familiar voice asked.

Jackson and Chris stared at their food. Tommy slowly turned his head. "Hi, Zach," he said in a meek voice.

"I think I'll take that pizza." Zach grabbed the slice from Tommy's tray. "You probably don't need this milk

93

either." He chugged down the carton and dumped a plate of green beans into Tommy's lap.

"Oops." Zach laughed. "I'm sorry."

Tommy pushed himself away from the table. "You know what?" He could feel his temper rising.

"What?" Zach stepped closer to Tommy.

Tommy looked at the hulking beast before him and changed his mind. "Nothing."

"Mr. Butler," a teacher interrupted, "you are not supposed to be here. Now say goodbye to your friends and get back to the suspension room."

"Goodbye, friends," Zach said sarcastically.

"So long." Jackson offered him a cheerful wave.

Zach walked away, looking around for other people to torment before leaving the cafeteria.

"I'm sick of this," Tommy said. "I wish we could..."

"What?" Chris asked.

"I don't know." If he thought about it, Tommy didn't really want to hurt Zach. He just wished he could scare him enough to make him quit bothering him and his friends. "We could dump him in the trash," he suggested.

Jackson and Chris started laughing, but no sooner had the words left Tommy's mouth than he felt a sharp pain in his leg. The medallion was burning his flesh.

Tommy sat up straight, unsure of what to do. He tried to reach into his pocket to remove the medallion, but the intensity of the heat prevented him from doing so. Tommy grimaced in pain as the medallion grew hotter.

Jackson noticed first. "Tommy, what's wrong?"

"I don't know." Tommy clenched his teeth in agony. "But the medallion is setting me on fire!" He slumped to one side.

"Then take it out!" Chris yelled.

With the pain growing worse by the second, Tommy reached into his pocket and pulled out the medallion. It burned his fingertips, but he wasn't able to let it go. The blue stone cast off florescent rays all around the cafeteria. Tommy's eyes blinked at the light's power. He tried to turn away from it, but couldn't.

All three boys sat transfixed by the unique blue beams scanning around the room, but no one else seemed to notice.

Then a loud scream coming from the hallway got everyone's attention. Zach staggered back into the lunchroom, covered in trash from the cafeteria. The students erupted with laughter and cheers.

Tommy looked at the medallion. The glowing blue stone faded and the heat disappeared. He quickly dropped it back into his pocket. He scanned the lunchroom, relieved that everyone had already resumed their earlier conversations.

"What just happened?" Chris asked.

"I don't know."

"Maybe that thing is magical after all," Jackson said.

Tommy watched as Zach was led out of the room, a long trail of trash following behind him.

"Well, if it is," Tommy said, "I like that kind of magic."

Everyone at the table smiled and agreed whole-heartedly.

The second-to-last period of the day was English. For Tommy, it was one of the most boring classes. Not that the teacher wasn't any good, but Tommy just didn't like the subject.

Five minutes into the "find a verb" lesson, the classroom phone rang. Tommy didn't move. The familiarity of school and the enjoyment of watching Zach Butler covered in garbage calmed him a bit, though he remained tense.

Mrs. Palmer spoke into the phone. "Yes, he is ... okay." She hung up and turned to Tommy. "They need you in the office."

All eyes watched Tommy as his stomach performed somersaults.

"Thanks, Mrs. Palmer." He stood up and walked slowly out of the classroom.

☆   ☆   ☆

Mrs. Palmer's room was located on the other side of Kennedy Middle School, so the long walk gave Tommy plenty of time to think about what awaited him in the office.

No one liked going to the office, Tommy thought. Nothing good ever happened when you were summoned there. More often than not, things just went from bad to worse or worst.

Tommy reached the end of the hallway and looked at the windowed office. The principal's door was closed. Then it finally hit Tommy: his Uncle Jack must be here. Relieved, he picked up his steps as he went down the hall.

Ms. Weathers, the secretary, directed Tommy to a chair while Principal Diggs finished with his business.

Tommy felt a smile creep across his face. He couldn't wait to see Uncle Jack, who would know how to handle the entire situation. Tommy thought that maybe Uncle Jack would take him on a treasure hunt. The idea brought a tingle to the back of Tommy's neck. For the first time he wasn't thinking about his pursuers or his father, just the fun and joy that came from seeing his uncle.

The door to the principal's office swung open and balding, overweight Mr. Diggs emerged.

Tommy smiled at him, but Mr. Diggs did not offer one in return. "Mr. Reed, please come in and have a seat."

Tommy stood and walked past the principal into the spacious office.

He stopped two steps inside the office. He didn't see his Uncle Jack sitting there. But he did see Gavin and Dillon.

"Hi there, Tommy," Gavin said. "Got a minute?"

FIFTEEN

A MAGICAL MOMENT

TOMMY'S HEART LEAPT IN his chest. The two so-called FBI agents sat before him in the one place Tommy never dreamed they would be: the principal's office. *Maybe they really were FBI agents*, he thought. *How else could they get in here?*

"Tommy, please sit down," Mr. Diggs said. Tommy sat in a cushioned chair as Mr. Diggs went behind his large oak desk. The principal left the door open.

"Now." Mr. Diggs cleared his throat before beginning his lecture. "It is my understanding that you have some information that these men, who, by the way, are FBI agents, need. Tommy, you have never been in trouble and I know that you want to do the right thing. It is your duty as an American and a student of this school to uphold the character traits that we consider important in building a society…"

Mr. Diggs continued, but Tommy tuned him out. His eyes darted around the room as he looked for an escape route. The expressions on Gavin and Dillon's faces gave Tommy pause; they must know he had the medallion, he thought. He found himself wishing for another trash dumping, but how many times could that happen? His mind pondered various ideas, all of which made him even more scared.

As Mr. Diggs droned on, Tommy began to consider handing over the medallion. It's really not magical, he thought, no matter what happened in the lunchroom with the glowing stone. Tommy looked out the window. Where was his Uncle Jack, anyway?

"So, finally," Mr. Diggs said, ending his long speech, "Tommy, could you please cooperate and give these gentlemen what they need?"

Tommy looked at Mr. Diggs and then at Gavin and Dillon as if seeing them for the first time.

"I'm sorry, what?"

"That's it." Dillon stood. Gavin put his arm out, and Dillon sat back down again.

"Tommy, all we need is what your uncle sent you," Gavin said. "Then we'll leave you alone and you can go on with your life."

"I showed you what he sent me," Tommy said. "Those buffalo coins. That's it."

Tommy slipped both hands into his pockets, gripping the medallion with the left one.

"Tommy." Dillon spoke with controlled fury. "We need the artifact. Your uncle stole it from an important excavation and made you an accomplice to his crime. We talked to your dad—"

"Which would lead you nowhere," Tommy said sarcastically.

"He knows your uncle a little better than you do, kid," Dillon said. "Now quit playing games!"

Tommy's anger grew as he thought of all the lies his father probably told them. He's just jealous, Tommy thought, because he never did anything with his life.

"If you aren't going to cooperate, then we have no choice but to place you under arrest," Gavin said.

"Arrest?" Tommy gripped the medallion tighter. If only he could disappear and find his Uncle Jack, all of this would be better. He needed to become invisible.

In the palm of his hand, Tommy felt the blue stone beginning to warm. Tommy started wishing harder for invisibility.

Tommy noticed the aghast looks on the three men's faces as they seemed to stare straight through him. Tommy looked around to see if he had missed something.

"Where did he go?" Dillon asked.

"Tommy, if this is some kind of trick you are only making it worse on yourself," Mr. Diggs said, rising from his seat. "It is time to stop this nonsense."

It took Tommy several seconds to realize the medallion had worked again. He'd vanished.

Mr. Diggs screamed for Ms. Weathers.

"Yes, sir?" She entered the room from the outer office. Seeing what might be his only chance to escape, Tommy bolted for the open door.

"Has Tommy Reed run or maybe crawled past your desk in the last ten seconds?"

"No, he hasn't."

I just did, Tommy thought as he made his way to the outside office door.

"If you see him, report to me immediately."

"Of course." Ms. Weathers turned to go back to her desk when suddenly she screeched, "There he is!"

Tommy looked at her and his blue eyes widened. Principal Diggs, Gavin, and Dillon ran to the doorway.

"Get him!" Gavin yelled.

Tommy opened the outer office door and sprinted down the hallway.

Gavin and Dillon nearly trampled Ms. Weathers as they toppled over her in their attempt to get to Tommy. They jumped up quickly and sprang after the young Mr. Reed.

SIXTEEN

DIAMOND ARRIVAL

TOMMY RAN AS IF his feet had wings. He tore down the steps to the cafeteria and ducked inside the boiler room, which was the home of the janitorial staff and their student helpers.

Tommy saw Marcus Evans, a student assistant, holding a dripping mop over a bucket of water.

"Marcus," Tommy wheezed, now out of breath.

"You in a hurry?"

"Sorta." Tommy glanced around for a place to hide. "There are some people following me and I can't let them find me."

"Mr. Diggs one of them?"

"Yes."

"Hate that guy," Marcus said. "Dude gives you detention just for punching a kid. Ain't that something? Hey man, hide by that last furnace over there. It'll be hot, but no one ever goes back that far and they won't be able to see you."

"Thanks." Tommy worked his way over pipes, old paint cans, and rusted volleyball poles until he reached the far furnace. He crouched down and wrapped his arms around his knees. The noise in the room would be good cover, Tommy thought. Still, he measured his breaths so they weren't too loud.

He stopped breathing when he heard the boiler room door burst open.

"Who is this?" Gavin asked.

"He's a student assistant," Mr. Diggs said. "Marcus, we are looking for Tommy Reed. Have you seen him?"

"No," Marcus said. "I was just getting a mop to clean up the cafeteria."

"If you see him, please report it to the office. It's very important." Mr. Diggs and Gavin ran through the cafeteria and back up the stairs.

*　　　*　　　*

"Old place look familiar?" Elizabeth asked as she and Jack drove toward Kennedy Middle School.

Jack shrugged. He really couldn't remember much about his hometown. Everything seemed new and yet at the same time oddly familiar, even though he hadn't been back to his home state in over a year. Or was it two?

"I just hope we can find Tommy," Jack said as they waited for the red light to change.

"You told him we were coming," Elizabeth said. "I am sure everything is fine. He's in school. What could happen?"

It took fifteen minutes for Jack and Elizabeth to drive from the small airport to Kennedy Middle School. Jack parked the car in the front lot and he and Elizabeth walked quickly to the front door.

103

"Did you go to school here too?" Elizabeth asked as they entered the main office.

"Yeah, but when I went here it was a high school instead of a middle school."

Ms. Weathers emerged from the office mailroom. "May I help you?" She sat back down behind her desk.

"We're here to see Tommy Reed," Jack said. "I'm his uncle."

Ms. Weathers shook her head. "He sure is popular today."

"What do you mean?"

"Well, two FBI agents and Mr. Diggs just had him in the office, and apparently. . ." Ms. Weathers looked around to see if anyone was listening before whispering, "he snuck out and 'disappeared,' according to Mr. Diggs."

"Disappeared?" Elizabeth looked at Jack.

"The medallion," Jack muttered beneath his breath. "Do you know where he is now?"

"They are looking for him in the building," Ms. Weathers said.

"Let's go." Jack pushed Elizabeth to the door leading to the main hallway.

"Hold it," Ms. Weathers screamed. "You are not allowed to run these hallways without permission from Principal Diggs, so if you would kindly take a seat before I call security, I will get him."

Jack and Elizabeth stopped moving and politely sat down.

"Never thought this would happen," Elizabeth said.

"What, the FBI guys being here?"

"No. That I'd be back in the principal's office."

      ✢   ✢   ✢

Tommy poked his head up and saw the door shut. Marcus continued wringing out the mop. Tommy worked his way back toward Marcus.

"Thanks."

"No problem," Marcus said. "I would never tell Mr. Diggs anything. The guy is an idiot."

"Yeah." Tommy's mind was racing with ideas. "Do you think you can get a message to Chris Henderson? He's in Mrs. Palmer's English class right now, room ten."

Marcus shrugged. "Sure, what's the message?"

"Hang on." Tommy unzipped his backpack.

He fished out a spiral notebook and opened it to a blank page, then began writing symbols in neat rows.

Marcus stared at the writing. "That's a message?"

"Yeah." Tommy finished jotting down the last symbol. "It's called monoalphabetic substitution cipher. It was used by the Freemasons during the Revolutionary War to encrypt their messages to hide them from the British."

"Oh," Marcus said, very unimpressed.

"Here, get this to Chris Henderson." Tommy ripped the piece of paper out of the notebook and handed it to Marcus.

"Consider it done," Marcus said. "Room ten?"

"Room ten." He watched Marcus leave the room.

Tommy headed back to his hiding place, praying the message would get to Chris.

The walkie-talkie on Mr. Diggs's belt crackled as Ms. Weathers's voice came through. "Mr. Diggs, please pick up."

Diggs smiled half-heartedly at Gavin and Dillon and pulled the walkie-talkie from his belt.

"Yes."

"I have a Jack Reed here to see Tommy. Have you found him yet?"

Gavin paused as the name registered in his mind.

"No, but we will continue looking." Diggs looked at Gavin and Dillon. "I could force the school into a lockdown mode and get the police here."

Gavin and Dillon's eyes grew wide. "No need for that," Gavin said. "As a matter of fact, we should be calling into headquarters with an update. Thank you for your time. We've already taken up enough of it."

"It's no trouble." Mr. Diggs noticed Marcus walking by. "Hey, Marcus, anything?"

"No," he said before continuing down the hallway to room ten.

"Who was that?" Dillon asked.

"Already talked with him," Gavin said dismissively. "Mr. Diggs, thanks for your help." He grabbed Dillon by the arm. "Let's go."

The two men walked down the stairs and out a side door near the bus port.

"Gentlemen, you can go out the front door," Mr. Diggs said as the glass door slammed shut.

After the men left, he held the walkie-talkie close to his mouth. "Tell Mr. Reed I'll be right there."

Gavin and Dillon ran to the car.

"Why did we get out of there so fast?" Dillon asked.

"Didn't you hear? The kid's Uncle Jack is in there."

"So Diamond Jack Reed is here." Dillon looked back at the school.

"Get in. We need to call Mr. Ernesto and explain the situation."

"Why?" Dillon climbed into the passenger seat.

"Because Reed is supposed to be dead. And since he's not, I think we have bigger problems."

The black Benz pulled out of the Kennedy Middle School parking lot and sped away.

Mr. Diggs came down the hallway and entered the main office.

"This is Jack Reed, Tommy's uncle," Ms. Weathers said. "And this is his aunt?"

"No," Elizabeth said. "I'm Elizabeth Haden, Jack's assistant."

Ms. Weathers rolled her eyes. "Of course you are."

"Please come into my office and we can talk," Mr. Diggs said.

Jack and Elizabeth walked into the office, and this time Mr. Diggs shut the door.

Marcus handed the note to Mrs. Palmer, who passed it on to Chris. Chris opened the folded piece of notebook paper and saw the symbols. He flashed it toward Shannon, who simply nodded her understanding.

Chris and Shannon huddled together in the hallway after class ended.

"Let me see." She grabbed the note.

"He used the cipher," Chris said. "You got the key?"

"Yeah." She looked at the symbols.

"Where are you next?" he asked.

"Math. You?" Shannon fished out a small spiral notebook from her backpack.

"Social Studies."

"Where's Jackson?" Shannon folded the paper in half.

"AP Chemistry," Chris said. "Since I've got Social Studies, give me the message and the key."

"Here." Shannon handed the note and notebook to Chris. "When you find out what it says, let me know."

"Okay." Chris hurried to Mr. Crist's Social Studies class.

✢   ✢   ✢

After checking the identification of Jack and Elizabeth, Mr. Diggs smiled. "How can I help you?" He sat down behind his enormous desk.

"I understand some men came to see Tommy today," Jack said.

108

"Yes, and I must tell you I was very disappointed in how Tommy reacted."

"Why?"

"I can't get into it, but the men were FBI agents and he refused to cooperate and answer their questions. That is very unlike him."

"Questions about what?" Jack asked.

"You," Diggs said bluntly. "Something that you sent him in the mail was a stolen artifact from some excavation."

"Stolen?" Jack looked surprised.

"Yes. The two gentlemen wanted it back."

"These FBI guys," Jack said, "did they give their names, or a card that lists where to reach them?"

Mr. Diggs smiled again. "I must tell you that I am reluctant to give you much information, Mr. Reed."

"Why is that?" Jack asked, annoyed.

"If you have done what they say, then you are a criminal. And I do not want to be an accomplice in any way."

The comment caused Jack to stand.

"Just tell me where Tommy is."

"I think we need to keep our temper," Mr. Diggs said, surprised by Jack's sudden burst of emotion.

"Are you going to tell me or not?"

Diggs waited a moment before answering. "We are still looking for him."

Jack turned to Elizabeth. "Let's go."

They started for the door, but Elizabeth stopped and walked back to Mr. Diggs's desk.

"You never said the names of the FBI agents or if they gave you a card." She flashed him her dazzling smile.

Mr. Diggs smiled back. "Gavin and Dorey or Darryl—or something like that."

"And a card?"

Diggs shook his head no.

"FBI agents with no cards," Elizabeth said. "That should have been your first red flag." She walked out the door with Jack.

Feeling slighted, Mr. Diggs yelled after her, "They did have badges!" But Jack and Elizabeth were already gone.

✻   ✻   ✻

Chris waited to decode the message until Mr. Crist started a movie. Opening the note from Tommy, Chris studied the symbols carefully.

He flipped through the notebook in the darkness until he came to the page with the key grid used to decipher this type of message by replacing letters with symbols. Tommy must have been in serious trouble, Chris thought, for him to use the cipher. Using the key, it took Chris several minutes to translate the code. He looked over the letters, stunned.

THEY R HERE.
BACK OF SCHOOL.
END OF DAY.

Chris closed the notebook, folded the paper, and put it into his pocket. Chris got up and asked Mr. Crist if he could use the restroom.

Mr. Crist, who was planning to retire at the end of the year, no longer cared if any students stayed in class or not, so he readily granted the request.

Chris walked to Shannon's math class and knocked on the door, waiting until Mrs. Stevenson opened it slightly.

"The office needs Shannon McDougal."

"Shannon," Mrs. Stevenson said. "Office."

Chris and Shannon walked a few steps down the hallway and stood beside some lockers out of view from passersby.

"Well?" Shannon asked in excitement. Chris handed her the note. He looked around nervously, as though waiting for the men to jump out at any moment.

Shannon read the note. "They're here? Those FBI guys?" She glanced around.

"Relax," Chris said. "When class is over we'll meet in the main hallway."

"Why?"

"Because Jackson will be finishing his AP class and we can all go out the gym doors. It's a shortcut to the back of the school."

"I guess," Shannon said.

"Scared?" Chris asked.

She straightened up. "Nope. You?"

"Ah." Chris walked away, not wanting Shannon to know about the knot in his stomach.

Shannon turned to go back to math feeling the same way.

The bell rang to signal the end of the school day, and Shannon and Chris grabbed their stuff from their lockers and hustled to the main hallway. They met Jackson and pulled him aside.

"Read this." Chris handed him Tommy's note.

Jackson's brown eyes blinked quickly behind his glasses. "Where are they?" He looked down the hallway.

"We don't know," Chris said, "but let's get behind the school as quickly as we can."

"Hey, where's your buddy?" Zach Butler yelled from the other side of the hall.

"None of your business, Zach," Shannon said.

Zach approached her, and for the first time he didn't seem intimidated.

"You don't scare me, Shannon."

"Zach, if I wanted to I could mop this floor with you and not even break a sweat."

Chris and Jackson stepped away as the two combatants faced each other.

"I'd like to see you try," Zach said.

Shannon's eyes narrowed and she clenched her fists. This would be fun, she thought, and then she remembered Tommy.

"I've got to go, but this isn't over." She turned to leave.

"I knew you weren't that tough." A broad smile slipped across Zach's face.

"Yes, I am," Shannon said, and then did a quick reversal and approached the smiling bully. She pulled back her right fist and slugged him in the gut.

Chris and Jackson looked at Shannon with a mixture of surprise and pride. Zach dropped to the ground like a sack of dirt.

Shannon stood over the fallen beast. "Don't ever bother me or my friends again."

Zach barely muttered a word as he gripped his stomach and prayed for relief.

Shannon looked at Chris and Jackson and winked. "Come on." The two followed her as she led the way.

The three Club members walked down the hall to the gym and made a quick left, exiting through a side door. They saw the bus port busy with students getting on their buses. Shannon, Chris, and Jackson scanned the crowd, hoping to find Tommy and at the same time trying to avoid his pursuers.

"You see him?" Jackson asked.

"No," Chris said. "But there are a lot of people out here."

Shannon looked across the street. "I don't see the black car either. Maybe they left."

"Guys." Tommy emerged from behind some bushes, drenched with sweat. His clothes stuck to his body like he had been playing in the rain.

"What happened to you?" Jackson asked.

"I'll explain later. We can't use my house, so we'll need to use the backup."

"My house," Shannon said, somewhat surprised. "Why?"

"Those FBI guys are sure to have someone at my house, but not yours."

"Never thought this would happen," Chris said.

"Then let's move," Shannon said.

The group blended into the crowds of kids as they boarded Shannon's bus.

Chris tapped Tommy, who slumped down beside him. "Where is your Uncle Jack?"

"I don't know," Tommy said. "But we sure could use his help right now."

SEVENTEEN

ANGER, RELUCTANCE, AND SURPRISES

SHANNON MCDOUGAL'S HOUSE STOOD in a cul-de-sac with four houses on each side. Her parents admired her toughness and strength of character and supported her in everything she did. They also didn't mind the time she spent with the other treasure hunters, though she was the only female member.

What Shannon's parents did not know was that their house was the official backup clubhouse for the Treasure Hunters Club.

The finished basement of the McDougal house had a traditional bar and entertainment center. Off in a separate room was Mr. McDougal's office, which had an elaborate computer system that could rival any software company. This became a real advantage to the Club members if they needed information in a hurry. However, they didn't like to use the second clubhouse for fear of Shannon's parents overhearing their meetings.

When the group arrived at Shannon's home, they scurried past Mrs. McDougal with a quick hello and ran to the basement, taking seats on an old multi-colored couch.

Tommy settled in and told the rest of the Club the story of his day. They sat mesmerized by the tale.

"You *disappeared?*" Shannon asked.

"That's impossible," Jackson added.

"I'm telling you, it happened. What about the trash thing with Zach?"

"What?" Shannon asked.

"You didn't hear?" Chris asked. "Tell her."

A broad smile crossed Tommy's face. "Well, Zach's all over me in the lunchroom. I'm getting mad, but I'm not going to do anything. I thought it would be funny if he was dumped in with the garbage."

"And it happened?" Shannon said in disbelief.

"Just crushed him with it," Tommy said. "But right before it happened, when I was wishing, I felt the stone in the medallion start to heat up and burn. When I took it out of my pocket, these blue lights were flying all over the place."

"What did everybody do?" Shannon asked.

"Nothing. It was like we were the only ones to see the light show . . . until Zach stumbled back in."

"That's one crazy story," Shannon said.

"All right then, what do we do now?" Chris wondered.

All eyes fell to Tommy.

"We need more information about this medallion." Tommy pulled it from his pocket. "I'm still not sure why my Uncle Jack would send this to me if he knew it might lead to trouble, but there is obviously something special about it."

"Maybe that's why he sent it," Chris said.

"Chris is right," Shannon said. "He probably thought it would be safer with you."

"What about him telling me to protect it from everyone?"

"He must have figured out—too late, unfortunately—that there was trouble associated with the medallion," Shannon said.

"By the way, out of curiosity, where *is* your uncle?" Jackson asked.

Jack waited impatiently at the stoplight. With his worst fears realized, he felt unsure of his next move. He cursed himself for not finding out more about Manual in the beginning, and now he'd put Tommy, someone he cared for, in danger.

"Do you have any ideas?" Jack asked. The light turned green.

"Yes, I do," Elizabeth said with confidence.

"What?" Jack seemed eager to hear her plan.

Elizabeth gave Jack an all-knowing look. It took Jack several seconds before he realized what this particular look meant.

"No," Jack said when he finally understood.

"Yes," Elizabeth insisted.

"No, no, no." Jack shook his head, emphasizing his disapproval.

"Why not?"

"Because it will be pointless. It always turns into a big fight, and I don't think we have the time to waste with him."

Elizabeth breathed deeply, collecting her thoughts.

"Jack, he is your brother whether you like it or not. His son is in trouble. It's your duty to tell him!"

"My brother doesn't care."

"He might. Besides, we need help finding Tommy. Maybe he has some ideas on where to look. We sure don't have any."

The car came to a stop sign, but Jack didn't accelerate again. He just sat mulling over Elizabeth's comments.

"Well?" she asked.

"Left to the house and right to ... I'm not sure." Jack smiled.

He waited for traffic to clear before turning left.

"I know this might be tough, but maybe it can bring the two of you closer together."

"There's too much history between us," Jack said. "And old grudges die hard in my family."

"We're still going to need his help finding Tommy."

"My brother can barely help himself, let alone help his son."

"We need him," Elizabeth insisted.

"Why is that? I mean, I understand telling him his son is in trouble, but do you really believe he knows anything?"

"He knows Tommy's friends," Elizabeth said. "I figure Tommy is with one of them."

"How do you know?"

"He's a teenager. He won't trust adults, so his friends are the only ones he'd talk to."

"I guess." Jack shrugged.

"How about his disappearing?" Elizabeth said.

"Yeah, that medallion must really be magical. No wonder Manuel wanted it so badly. That means the myth is real."

"Do you think Juan and Conrado ever made it back to shore?"

"I would say no, and Manuel's probably not very happy about it. I'm guessing that's why those two guys are after Tommy. I was so stupid to leave the UPS receipt out in the open."

"It wasn't your fault, Jack. I never trusted Manuel from the start."

They drove in silence for several more miles. Finally, Elizabeth patted Jack on the knee.

"We'll find him," she said, hoping to reassure Jack and, more importantly, herself.

✵   ✵   ✵

Manuel answered his cellphone after the second ring. It was Gavin. As Manuel listened, he grew angry. How could two of his top people fail to handle a teenage boy?

"So what do you plan to do?" Manuel asked.

"Well," Gavin stammered, sensing the disappointment in Manuel's tone. Gavin's next statement

119

caused him to tremble for fear of Manuel's reaction. "There is something else."

"Of course there is." Manuel sounded disgusted. "What is it?"

"Diamond Jack Reed is here."

There was silence on the line. Manuel could not believe it. That could only mean that his bodyguards, whom he trusted to take care of Jack and his assistant, were either lost at sea or dead.

"I see," Manuel said softly.

Neither man spoke for a few moments. Gavin started mumbling something about revenge, but Manuel cut him off.

"It seems I must take care of this personally. I will be on my plane later today. Please be at the airport to pick me up."

Manuel threw his phone across the room. "I hate you, Jack Reed!" he screamed.

"He'll be here tonight." Gavin looked at Dillon in disgust and put his phone away.

Jack pulled the car into the driveway and stopped.

"I can't do this."

"Sure you can," Elizabeth reassured him.

"He and I will end up fighting, and it's always about the past and all that. I'm not doing it."

Elizabeth had finally heard enough. "Then don't!" she yelled. "Jack, I have listened to stories about your brother and I have been sympathetic, but this isn't about the two of you. Tommy is in trouble and he needs our help. So suck it up, swallow your pride, and let's go and ask your brother for help finding his son. If you can't man up, then I'll do it myself!"

Jack was flabbergasted. She had never spoken to him like this, and yet he knew she was right. Manuel and his goons would continue to dog Tommy until they got what they wanted, and Jack knew they wouldn't hesitate to kill anyone who dared to stand in their way.

He turned the key and the car shut off.

"Good," she said. "Come on." She got out of the car and headed for the front door.

As she walked up the two steps to the porch, Elizabeth looked back over her shoulder. Jack wavered in the driveway. Elizabeth motioned for him.

Reluctantly he walked up to the porch. He tried to smile. "This is about Tommy."

Elizabeth nodded and knocked on the door.

*   *   *

The Gulf Stream jet took off just after four p.m. Manuel's pilots informed him they should arrive around seven o'clock that evening, weather permitting.

Manuel sat by himself and stared out the window. With Jack back in the picture, he knew things had become much more complicated. Manuel wondered if Jack realized the awesome power the medallion possessed. More importantly, would he know how to use it? And what of this teenage punk who was able to elude one of his best hit teams? He needed someone new, someone who could handle

121

this situation without Manuel's guidance. Someone who could disappear without a trace after the job was done.

Manuel pulled his cellphone from his pocket and punched some numbers. He waited until he heard a male voice say, "Hello."

"Yes," Manuel said. "I did not think you would be needed, but I was wrong ... tonight after seven ... no problem." Manuel closed his phone and, for a brief moment, felt relief.

Unshaven, clothes dirty, and holding a beer can, Eric Reed opened the door and stood before his brother and Elizabeth. He shook his head in amazement.

"Boy, you must be in real trouble if you came here." He laughed. "Milly," he called, "come and see what the wind blew in."

Milly came out from the kitchen and forced a smile.

"Hello, Jack. What a pleasant surprise. Please come in."

"Yeah," Eric said, "by all means come in."

Jack and Elizabeth walked inside and stood in silence. Eric shut the door and walked past them into the family room. He took a slug of beer and plopped down onto his recliner.

"I'm sorry," Jack said, embarrassed. "Milly, this is Elizabeth."

"Nice to meet you," Milly said.

"Like-wise."

"Can I get you two anything? Coffee, tea, a pop?"

"We're fine," Jack said.

"Well sit down," Eric yelled from the next room. "Tell us about the trouble that brought you back here."

"I'm not in any trouble, Eric," Jack snapped.

"You're the rich one, so you can't possibly need money. From the look on your face you know we don't have any."

"I don't have a look," Jack said, growing impatient. He entered the family room. "Now that you mention it, how about getting off your lazy butt and—"

"You calling me lazy in my own house?" Eric stood up from his chair, his fists clenched.

"Right now I am." Jack faced his brother.

Elizabeth stepped between them. "All right, that's enough of this from both of you. Now sit down."

The brothers stared at one another for several moments before obeying.

"Thank you," Elizabeth said. "Now, I am sure that you two have plenty to talk about, but that is for another time. We need to know where Tommy is."

"You got him mixed up in your life?" Eric shook his head. "That's why he's wanted by those two FBI guys."

"They are not FBI agents," Jack said.

"Well, they had badges."

"Sure they weren't plastic toys?" Jack's voice was sarcastic.

"You know, you're not so big that I still couldn't whip your butt," Eric said.

123

"Eric." Elizabeth stepped in again. "Do you know where Tommy is?"

"Spent the night at a friend's house. Not sure whose."

"Chris Henderson," Milly said softly.

"Do you know where he lives?" Elizabeth asked.

Embarrassed, Milly just shook her head.

"Eric," Jack pleaded, "your son's life is on the line here. Please give me something to help him."

After a long pause, Eric said, "If Tommy found himself in trouble, he would come to me. He's always in that old camper out back. He's got it locked up pretty good, but if you can get in there you might find something."

"Thanks," Jack said.

"Milly, show them where it is." Eric cracked open another beer. "My boy knows how to take care of himself. I did teach him something, you know."

Elizabeth and Jack followed Milly through the kitchen and out the back door.

"Is Tommy gonna be all right?" Milly asked, her eyes welling with tears.

"Yes, Milly," Jack said. "I won't let anything happen to him."

"Jack, about Eric." Milly shook her head.

Jack raised his hand. "It's not your fault, Milly. That stuff goes back a long way between the two of us."

Milly put her hand on Jack's and squeezed it before walking back into the house.

Jack turned to Elizabeth. "Let's go in and find something useful."

✿ ✿ ✿

Tommy and Shannon worked on her father's computer while Chris and Jackson studied the medallion.

"Nothing," Shannon said, frustrated.

"Keep at it," Tommy encouraged.

"I keep getting websites about strange magic, but the articles make no sense and are written by amateurs. You can forget about any information that has to do with those symbols. They don't exist."

"What about hurricanes and bad storms, stuff like that?" Tommy asked.

"According to a site about the history of Port Royal Harbor, sixteen major hurricanes were reported between 1712 and 1951. So we know there were bad storms, but it wasn't like the people in Jamaica kept accurate records. There could have been more than sixteen. There's no mention of any medallions." Shannon shrugged her shoulders.

Tommy stared at his computer screen, unsure of what to do next. Even though the dates seemed familiar to him, he couldn't place them.

On the other side of the basement, Jackson wrote out the symbols on large sheets of paper and studied each one.

"Is that helping?" Chris asked.

"Just give me a minute."

Jackson couldn't comprehend the symbols. They didn't seem to come from any time period he knew about. The problem had him stumped and frustrated.

Finally, he blurted out, "They just don't make sense!"

"Maybe they aren't supposed to," Chris said.

"What?"

"I mean, maybe they were just carved there so the medallions would have symbols."

"No." Jackson shook his head. "How do you explain the strange things that happen with it? Those symbols mean something magical, and we need to find out what it is."

"Ahh," Shannon yelled from the computer room. "Nothing!"

Silence pervaded the room. The adventure the group had always wished for ended up being nothing like what they'd imagined. People were trying to get them, maybe even kill them, and their sense of helplessness caused them all to feel deep frustration.

Tommy remembered things his uncle had told him about treasure hunting, and felt a sudden surge of energy to fight on.

"Guys," Tommy said, "my uncle always said 'when the puzzle proves too great, that's when a real treasure hunter will emerge.' We've got to dig in and keep going. The answer is out there just waiting to be found, but it isn't going to be easy."

Tommy's words and the look of determination on his face gave the rest of the Club a renewed sense of purpose. They pressed on.

"Try this." He leaned over and typed a word into the search engine for Shannon to see.

Chris saw his friend's newfound excitement and followed suit. "Let's start over," he said to Jackson.

The group started working again and reaffirmed what they already knew about one another: no matter the problem, they would always keep trying.

✳   ✳   ✳

Jack examined the keypad lock and smiled. *Couldn't have done better myself*, he thought.

Using a thin metal rod, he poked around inside the lock. He turned it several times until he heard a click and saw the green light flashing.

"And I thought we'd have to break it down," Elizabeth said as she walked through the door.

Once inside, the veteran treasure hunters looked in amazement at the setup.

"This is nicer than ours," Elizabeth said.

"Look at this." Jack stared at a wall adorned with maps. "Tommy marked everywhere I've been."

"What's all this?" Elizabeth pointed to a shelf filled with small artifacts.

"Some of the stuff I've sent him over the years." Jack grabbed an old Spanish coin and smiled. "Remember this?"

"Sure," Elizabeth said. "It was my first dredge."

127

"Seems so long ago."

"It was, Jack," Elizabeth said strongly.

They looked around the camper for several more minutes, but found nothing.

"Kid's got some great books," Elizabeth said as she admired the small library.

"Any address books?" Jack asked.

"I don't see any."

Jack glanced at a photo on the wall. He grabbed it and stared at the faces. These must be the people Tommy talks about, Jack thought. In the picture, three young people stood next to Tommy, who was holding a pink soda can that said TAB. Jack smiled, wondering if they still made that drink. He turned the picture over and read the inscription. "Our first treasure find: Treasure Hunters Club: Tommy, Chris, Jackson, and Shannon."

"It's them." Jack showed the picture to Elizabeth.

"Just the first names," Elizabeth said as she took the frame.

Jack grabbed a book off the shelf. "Here is their yearbook. See if you can match the pictures with the names."

"Sounds like fun," Elizabeth said.

"Then get the names of their parents and use that computer to find them."

Elizabeth flipped through the pages quickly, her eyes scanning the pictures.

"Done," she said with a satisfied smile.

"You sure do work fast." Jack looked impressed.

"I know," she said, sitting down at the computer and clicking her way to a search engine. She started typing.

"What are you doing?"

"The system has a security wall, so I'm circumventing it."

It took Elizabeth five minutes to find all of the Treasure Hunters Club parents. An Internet White Pages site listed their phone numbers and addresses. Elizabeth turned off the computer and motioned for Jack to follow her out the door.

"Let's go and find your nephew," she said confidently.

EIGHTEEN

MANUEL ARRIVES

GAVIN AND DILLON WAITED in a large hangar at the far end of the small airport. All private charters came this way since most millionaires and billionaires didn't have time to deal with airline security measures.

The Gulf Stream V taxied its way to a stop. After a few moments, the door dropped open and out stepped Manuel de la Ernesto. He did not look happy.

"Señor Ernesto, so good to see you again," Gavin said.

Manuel eyed Gavin and Dillon with disgust. "If you two had done your job, I wouldn't have to be here."

"Our car will take you to the motel." Gavin opened the back door while Dillon gathered Manuel's luggage from the plane. "It's pretty primitive out here."

Once Manuel was seated in the car, they headed for the exit.

"I am sure I don't have to tell you how disappointed I am with you both," Manuel said. "I have lost two of my best men, and you tell me that the medallion, which was within my grasp, is still being held by some kid!" Manuel clenched his teeth. "I should have you both killed."

"We were sorry to hear about Juan and Conrado, Mr. Ernesto, but we have a plan that will get the medallion back in our hands."

"And what is that?"

"It seems Tommy Reed hangs out with a group of friends—three, to be exact—and we figure by putting the heat on them, he'll easily give up the medallion."

"And what about Jack Reed?"

"Well." Gavin looked at Dillon, who shrugged.

"Mr. Ernesto," Dillon said. "We thought maybe he would realize his nephew is in danger and back off."

Manuel laughed.

"You obviously do not know Jack Reed."

"Yes, sir," Gavin said. "I think we do and—"

"I have heard enough of this," Manuel said, cutting him off. "Gentlemen, it is time to call in a professional, a man who can get things done and not leave a trace. Someone with a way of blending into the background after a job is finished. A real professional."

"Who is that?" Dillon asked.

"Slider."

Gavin and Dillon looked at each another.

"Do we need to take such a drastic step?" Gavin asked.

"He's right, sir," Dillon said. "We can handle this."

"I don't believe it. Besides, Slider and Jack Reed have such a lovely history. It would be so nice to bring the two of them together again."

"They know each other?" Gavin asked.

"For years. Slider would have been greater than the famous Diamond Jack Reed if not for a quirk of fate. Slider found himself about one hundred yards away from one of the greatest silver bar caches in the west, but Jack beat him to it. Jack's legend grew larger while Slider slipped into obscurity. That was, of course, before he took up his new profession of quietly fixing people's problems."

"That's one way to put it," Dillon said sarcastically.

"He considers himself a problem solver," Manuel corrected, "and we need this kind of problem solved."

"I still don't think we need Slider," Dillon said.

Manuel waited a few moments before he spoke.

"Gentlemen, Slider will be much more motivated than the two of you. Your services will certainly be needed, but this time as decoys. Slider will handle the more dangerous acts. You don't understand the importance of this medallion. It is time to turn up the pressure on this kid." Manuel smirked. "And his uncle, too."

The men did not talk the rest of the way to the motel.

Gavin pulled the car to the front of the motel, and Dillon stepped out to help Manuel.

Manuel got out of the car and grunted, "Get my bags," before walking into the lobby.

Dillon waited for Gavin to open the trunk and then grabbed the luggage.

As the two walked side by side into the hotel, Dillon leaned over toward Gavin. "If he's calling in Slider, how are we supposed to help?"

"I don't know," Gavin said. "Let's just hope Slider lets us."

"Is he really that good?"

"I've never met him, but the stories I've heard about him are quite impressive."

NINETEEN

DECISIONS

"WELL THAT'S THE BEST I can do," Shannon said, and threw an encyclopedia on top of the pile of reference books surrounding her.

"I can't believe we aren't able to find any more information than the basics," Tommy said. "Anything with you, Chris?"

"I'm tapped. But Jackson isn't finished trying."

Jackson Miller's genius was being put to the test. He loved moments like these, but the frustration of not being able to solve this puzzle angered him.

"Why not just go to the police?" Shannon said.

"With what?" Tommy mocked a conversation. "Yes, Officer, I have a magical medallion that two men are trying to kill me for."

"Don't think they'd believe you?" Shannon asked with a smile.

"I think when someone hears the word 'magical' in a sentence, they tune you out."

"We could go to your parents," Chris suggested.

Tommy looked at his good friend. "I'm sorry, Chris, but have you met my parents?"

Chris thought about it for a moment. "I guess you're right. I'm sorry for bringing it up."

"What about Uncle Jack? Isn't he supposed to be on his way?" Shannon asked.

"He was, but I don't know where he is. And now that my cell is broken I have no way of getting in touch with him."

"Why not just use one of our phones?" Shannon suggested.

"I could, but my Uncle Jack's cell number was in my phone and I don't remember it."

"You can't remember it?" Shannon smiled.

Annoyed, Tommy said, "No, I can't."

"Why don't you ask your parents?"

"My dad doesn't exactly love his brother, and I wouldn't want to put my mom in that kind of situation."

"I guess." Shannon shrugged.

"Hey guys," Jackson called from across the room. He stared at the computer screen and waved his hand to the others. "I think you need to see this."

"What is it?" Tommy asked as Shannon and Chris followed him to Jackson's work area.

"It's a website for mythological artifacts."

"Yeah, so?" Chris asked.

"So?" Jackson looked annoyed. "Look." He pointed at the computer screen. A picture of the blue-stoned medallion filled the monitor.

"Is that it?" Shannon asked.

"Sorta," Jackson said.

"What do you mean, sorta?"

"This place only deals with replicas of mythological artifacts."

"What does it say about the medallion?" Shannon asked.

"Nothing. The website is under construction, but maybe we can find an email or something?"

"Wait a second." Chris's eyes widened. "The Exhibit of Mythological Artifacts. Tommy, we saw this medallion there, remember? There was an entire display of medallions."

Tommy thought for a moment. "We saw Thor's hammer, the iron sword that can fight without a man, Achilles' shield, and those arrows used by the Roman god for something, but I really don't remember any medallion display."

"It was right before that security guy said we had to leave," Chris said.

Tommy pictured himself and Chris walking around and remembered seeing a table, but were there medallions on it? Then his eyes widened. "I remember now! They had a bunch of them."

"That's where we can get the information," Jackson said. "We can see if they have a duplicate of your medallion."

"Even if the museum doesn't have a duplicate, maybe someone at the exhibit will know what the markings mean," Shannon said.

"I think it's time we take a trip to the exhibit," Jackson said.

"What's the house number?" Jack asked Elizabeth.

"Fifty-five fifty-one."

"There it is." Jack pointed out the window and parked the car next to the curb.

They got out and headed for the front door.

"Let's handle this better than the Hendersons and the Millers," Elizabeth said.

"Hey, I thought they were lying and I didn't like their attitude."

"You threatened them."

"Yeah, well," Jack stammered, "they weren't very nice."

"Be that as it may," Elizabeth said, "I will do the talking to the McDougals."

Elizabeth approached the door and rang the bell.

"This has got to be it," Jack said.

"It better be," Elizabeth said. "This is the last house."

✲　　　✲　　　✲

In the McDougal basement, all of the young treasure hunters shouted out ideas about what to do with the medallion until Shannon finally had enough.

"That's it!" she yelled. "How long will it take us to get to the Civic Center?"

"I'd say thirty minutes," Tommy said, "but that's if we take the main roads."

"Okay, then, thirty minutes." Shannon stood up.

"Wait a second," Chris said. "If we take the main roads, those FBI guys are sure to see us."

"He's right," Jackson said.

"How much more time would it take us if we took the back roads?" Shannon asked.

"Another fifteen or twenty minutes," Tommy said.

"So an hour?"

"Looks like it."

Shannon had just started up the stairs to tell her mom she would be leaving when she heard a man's voice ask for Tommy. She stopped and ran back down the steps.

"There are people at the door."

"It's those FBI guys," Tommy said.

Shannon looked at Tommy. "What do we do?"

"The walk-out." Tommy pointed to a door that led to the McDougal backyard.

"Bikes are on the side of the house," Chris said.

"We can cut through the Torrences' yard and avoid the main streets," Jackson said.

Quietly, the group walked out the door and went for their bikes.

Meanwhile, Mrs. McDougal shifted on her feet nervously. "What is it you want with Tommy? And how is my daughter involved?"

"I am sorry, Mrs. McDougal, but my nephew is one of her friends and I need to know where he is."

"Tommy Reed is your nephew?"

"Yes," Jack said.

"You're the Uncle Jack or, what was it? Diamond Jack?"

Jack smiled. "Yes, that's right."

"Why didn't you say so?" She laughed. "I have heard so much about you from Shannon. You are quite the super hero."

"Thank you, but if we could just see Tommy," Jack said.

"No problem. Come on. I'll show you where they are."

Elizabeth and Jack followed Mrs. McDougal to the basement.

As they descended the stairs, she said, "They don't spend too much time here, but when they do, they come down to the basement and—" She stopped.

No one was there.

"They were just here," she insisted.

"Where did they go?" Elizabeth asked.

"They must have gone out the side door."

"To where?" Jack asked.

"Don't know," Mrs. McDougal said. "When they get on those bikes they could end up anywhere."

"Bikes?" Elizabeth looked at Jack. "They can't get too far."

Without another word, Jack and Elizabeth sprinted up the stairs and out the front door.

✢   ✢   ✢

Jack made a left onto Main Street and drove the speed limit while looking out his window.

139

"We are never going to find them."

"We will." Elizabeth scanned her side of the street.

"Elizabeth, we don't even know where to look. And if they're on their bikes, then they know every little side road and shortcut around this town."

"Isn't this your town, too? You should know the streets."

"It's been a long time," Jack said.

"Well, you better come up with something because time is running out."

"I know," he said. "I know."

The car moved forward as Jack and Elizabeth sat in silence, unsure where to turn next.

TWENTY

A NEW PLAYER

GAVIN SLOWED THE CAR to a stop in front of a warehouse in the downtown district.

"This is where he lives?"

"Works," Manuel corrected.

Gavin, Dillon, and Manuel got out of the car and walked to the front door. A small security camera in the corner of the doorway locked in on them.

"Can I help you?" a voice called from the intercom.

"We are here to see Slider. It's Manuel."

A buzzer sounded and the front door clicked open.

Dillon pushed on the door, and Manuel walked inside as the other two followed.

The large room did not look inviting. The lights were dim, reminding Gavin of a haunted house during Halloween. Four large television screens surrounded a console in the middle of the room. Multiple sonar and tracking systems were set up showing grids of the city. No one was in the room.

Dillon, a bit nervous, put his hand on his revolver as he walked into the room.

"Sit down." A bold, synthesized voice pierced the air.

The men sat on three chairs facing the computer console.

"To what do I owe the honor of this visit, Manuel?"

"Well, Slider, we have a problem." Manuel addressed the blank computer screen.

"Looks to me like *you* have the problem, not *we*," said the bold voice.

"Yes," Manuel agreed. "I need someone to get a medallion back to me that was stolen. A teenage boy has it. My team here seems to have scared the boy, and he is now on the run."

"Boys do not run far," Slider said. "What about his parents?"

Gavin took that question. "I don't think he would go there. The father isn't really interested in him, and the mother is afraid of her own shadow."

"Why call on me, Manuel?" Slider's electronic voice asked. "I mean, a kid has brought you here? Kind of embarrassing, isn't it?"

"That's true. It is embarrassing, but you might be interested in this boy's extended family."

"It matters?" Slider mocked.

"It does when he's Jack Reed's nephew."

"Diamond Jack Reed?" Slider's voice showed much more interest.

"One and the same," Manuel said. "In fact, he's here in town looking for his nephew as we speak."

A long silence followed, during which Gavin and Dillon shifted in their seats uncomfortably.

142

"I don't think I need to tell you what happens if Jack finds the boy and the medallion before we do," Manuel said.

Gavin and Dillon leaned back in their chairs, watching as a large figure appeared before them. He was dressed all in black with short hair and dark, unrevealing eyes.

"So nice of you to come out," Manuel said.

"Jack and I go way back."

"I know. Quite the rivalry, wasn't it?"

"It was until he stole from me," Slider said. "All these years I have waited. I'm glad you brought this to my attention."

"Let's put our priorities in line," Manuel said. "First the medallion, then Jack Reed. But remember, the medallion comes first."

"Okay then. It's obvious this kid— what's his name?"

"Tommy," Gavin said.

"Tommy has run to some friends for help. He's what, thirteen? Fourteen? His parents don't understand him. All kids his age feel that way, which is why he would turn to his friends first. If he has the medallion, where would he and his friends go? Has he seen anything from the medallion?"

Dillon moved slightly in his chair. "He did disappear on us once."

"Disappeared?" Slider asked, surprised.

"Yeah," Gavin said, "right in front of us. Just poof ... gone."

"So suffice to say he knows that the medallion is magical. But finding information about the artifact will be hard. The material he does find will be sketchy because he won't know where to look."

Slider started to pace the room as he continued to think out loud. "Where could he find information about the medallion that's not readily available on the Internet or the ..." He stopped pacing. "I know where he is."

"Where?" Manuel asked excitedly.

"The Exhibit of Mythological Artifacts."

"Why?" Dillon asked.

"It's the only place for him to go. It has been advertised in the local newspaper for weeks. The artifacts on display are from legends and folk tales. He will be looking for a replica of the medallion and the information that goes with it."

"Where is the exhibit?" Manuel asked.

"The Civic Center. But we are going to need more men."

"Not a problem," Manuel said.

"Then we'll go to the exhibit and wait for the kid to arrive. If the famous Diamond Jack Reed should be there, too, we can kill two birds with one shot."

"You mean stone," Gavin corrected. "Two birds with one stone."

Slider gave Gavin an icy glare. "No, I meant what I said."

Gavin looked at Dillon and nodded. "Okay, we'll get the car."

Once in the car, Gavin couldn't hold his tongue any longer. The idea of involving more men in this mission upset him. He cherished his job and didn't like when others told him how to do it. And it became even more important when money was involved.

"Boss, you know that Dillon and I are perfectly capable of getting this kid," Gavin said. "I mean, I understand about bringing in Slider, but do we really need more men?"

Manuel had his phone to his ear. "If Slider thinks they are needed, then we will do it. You will not receive any less money, Gavin, so don't worry. Once the medallion is in my possession, your money will come." The line picked up and Manuel said into his phone, "Yes, this is Manuel ... thank you."

Manuel looked at Gavin. "You are still important to this." Gavin nodded, but still felt angry about the entire situation.

"I am going to need a four-man tracker team," Manuel said into his cellphone. "When? Immediately. I have already talked with Slider." There was short pause, and then Manuel smiled. "Good, *gracias.*"

"Back to the motel?" Gavin asked.

"No, no," Manuel said. "The Civic Center, Gavin, the Civic Center."

✿   ✿   ✿

Jack tried to enjoy his cheeseburger, but his mind prevented it. Elizabeth ate a Caesar salad, which, from Jack's view, looked really healthy but was something to be avoided.

"Food is good." Elizabeth wiped her mouth.

"Best burgers in town." Jack dipped a grease-soaked fry into some ketchup.

"We've been here for half an hour. You got any ideas about your nephew?"

"Not one," Jack said as he opened a local newspaper.

"Anything good in there?"

"Boring townie stuff." Jack spread the paper over the table to scan both pages.

That's when Elizabeth saw the ad. "Mythological Artifacts Exhibit at the Civic Center." The words shot through Elizabeth's mind as Jack turned the page.

"I got it."

"What?" Jack asked, surprised.

"Look." Elizabeth grabbed for the paper, turned back to the advertisement, and pointed.

Jack's eyes read quickly and he smiled. "That's it," he said, "let's go."

Jack threw a twenty-dollar bill on the table and headed for the door, Elizabeth right behind him.

"How far away is the Civic Center?" she asked.

"We'll be there in fifteen minutes."

TWENTY-ONE

PEDALING FOR THEIR LIVES

THE TREASURE HUNTERS CLUB pedaled fast as they swept down a hill through another suburban neighborhood. The one thing Tommy forgot about when taking the back roads was all of the hills.

"How much farther?" Jackson asked as sweat dripped from his face.

"A ways," Tommy said.

"It feels like we've been out here forever," Shannon added.

"Longer." Chris, who was bringing up the rear, looked exhausted.

Part of the problem came from Tommy's insistence on hiding every time a car drove past. Although it did allow the kids much needed time to rest. All of the stops made for a long trip, which pushed the young treasure hunters anxiety level to new heights.

"Tommy," Chris yelled, "I need a break."

Tommy slowed his bike and it skidded to a stop at a corner. He waited for the others to catch up.

"We just took a break."

Sweat poured down Chris's face and he gasped for breath. "I just need some water or something."

"We don't have time."

Shannon looked at Chris. "I could probably use some water."

"Me too," Jackson said. "Tommy, it's not going to hurt our time or anything. We'll go to Lou's."

Tommy shook his head but agreed.

At a much slower pace, the four bikes made their way around a bend and pulled onto the sidewalk of Lou's Convenience Store.

Lou Bagarenio had run his own store for over thirty years. He loved the location in a neighborhood where kids and families could walk to get whatever they needed. He was well-known for his homemade ice cream and freshly baked bread.

Chris moved faster than he had all day. He dropped his bike, flung open the door, and headed for the bottled water.

"You'd think he was a water buffalo," Tommy said.

"I think a water buffalo is tougher than Chris," Shannon whispered.

The others walked inside and waved to the owner. Lou stood behind the counter wearing a dirty apron. As messy as Lou looked, his store was always immaculate.

"Chris, are you okay?" Shannon asked.

"Ahh." Chris held up the water after taking a prolonged drink. "This might be the greatest water I have ever tasted."

"What are you getting?" Jackson asked Shannon and Tommy.

"Fruit punch." Shannon said.

"Orange drink."

The three grabbed plastic bottles from the coolers and paid Lou. Chris paid for the bottle of water he already drank and purchased another one for the road.

"Hot out there?" Lou asked, grinning as he cleaned his hands on a checkered towel.

"Hi, Lou. Yeah, a little bit," Tommy said, and the rest nodded in agreement.

"Do you want anything else?" Lou looked around at the club members.

"Are we getting any food?" Chris asked.

"I don't have any more money." Shannon said.

"Me neither," Jackson said.

Chris looked at Tommy, who was staring at the magazine rack. "Tommy? Tommy!" He raised his voice.

"What?" Tommy looked surprised at Chris's tone of voice.

"Are you getting any food?"

"No. Lou, can I use the bathroom?"

"Sure. Just turn off the light when you're done."

"I'll meet you guys out front." Tommy headed for the back of the store.

"I think I have enough money for one candy bar." Chris scanned his remaining change.

Shannon and Jackson shook their heads.

After Chris bought his candy bar, the three walked outside. A blue car pulled up to the sidewalk and four men stepped out. They didn't speak. They grabbed the three youngsters and held them.

"Get the bikes," one of the larger men instructed another.

"Who are you?" Shannon struggled to free herself.

"FBI."

✳   ✳   ✳

Inside the bathroom, Tommy washed his hands and walked through the store. He waved at Lou, who was busy slicing pieces of roast beef for his deli.

"Tommy, have a good one," Lou said.

"Thanks, Lou, I'll see you later." Tommy pushed open the glass door and walked out.

As soon as Tommy's foot touched the sidewalk, he heard Shannon yell, "Run, Tommy, they're here!"

Tommy saw two men holding Shannon, Jackson, and Chris. He bolted for the bikes. One large man guarded two of the bikes while a smaller accomplice watched Tommy approach.

Tommy threw his hands out, shoving the smaller man to the ground as the bikes fell.

Tommy picked up one of the bikes, unsure whether it was even his, jumped on,, and started pedaling.

The larger man lunged at him, but missed and landed face first on the ground. Tommy started up the road as the two goons followed on foot.

Tommy felt like he was riding through mud. *I've got to go faster*, he thought. He repeated it to himself over and over again: *faster, faster; I've got to go faster*. In his pocket, he felt the familiar burn from the medallion searing into his leg. He yelled out in pain.

Suddenly his feet were moving beyond himself and he felt the bike lifting off the ground. He was no longer pedaling on pavement, instead spinning his wheels in the air. He was flying. The bike blasted away in a blaze of fire and smoke, leaving his pursuers in the dust.

The two men stopped as Tommy disappeared between the treetops.

"Call Slider," one of them said. "Tell him we've got the friends but lost the kid."

The smaller man flipped open his cellphone and hit a button.

Tommy's eyes bugged out of his face as he hung onto his bike, now a flying machine. The medallion's bright lights flashed through the sky as Tommy leaned left and right, dipping and dropping his way around trees and power lines. He wasn't sure how he was going to land, but as he climbed higher into the sky his eyes scanned out over his town. For a moment, Tommy felt at peace with the wind blowing through his hair. He didn't notice that the power from the medallion was fading.

Suddenly, the bike jerked, and Tommy began rapidly descending. He tried to turn the handlebars, but they were locked. He ducked his head as the bike flew into the trees. Leaves and branches whipped at Tommy's face as he tried to steady the bike.

151

Tommy squeezed the handlebars tightly as the ground came into view faster than he expected. The front tire hit first with a jarring jolt that sent Tommy hurtling over the handlebars.

He screamed as the force propelled his body into a bush. Tommy slowly opened his eyes and looked around. He checked his body to see if anything was broken and, when he felt ready, rolled out of the bush. Tommy was never so happy to feel grass on his face.

Tommy walked over to the bike. Despite the rough landing, Tommy didn't see any damage, much like his own body. He reached into his pocket and pulled out the medallion.

How does this thing do that? he wondered.

Tommy stared down the road, knowing that all of the answers were only a mile away. But he felt a strange emptiness creeping over him. He'd have to continue on alone. As a treasure hunter, Tommy knew going forward was the only way to solve the problem. As a friend, he was afraid for the other Club members and for himself. All of the doubts he'd ever had about this hunt came flashing back to him. He needed to carry on for his friends, as they would surely do for him.

Tommy got on the bike, pushed the pedal forward, and rode the old-fashioned way toward the Civic Center.

✻   ✻   ✻

Manuel, Gavin, and Dillon sat in the car eating tacos and waiting. Though he was not a man of patience,

Manuel showed a remarkable ability to exercise the virtue when needed.

"What are we waiting for?" Dillon asked, his mouth full of food.

Manuel sat in the backseat of the Mercedes while Gavin and Dillon sat up front.

"Slider said the kid would show up here," Manuel said.

"How does he know?" Gavin sounded annoyed. "We are putting an awful lot of trust in this guy—and money, sir, don't forget the money—for what may be a chance encounter. I find it hard to believe he's just going to walk across the ..." Gavin stopped talking.

Dillon's eyes perked up when he saw it too.

Gavin turned to his boss. "I can't believe I'm saying this, but there goes Tommy Reed, riding his bike across the street."

Manuel looked out the car window, seething at the sight of the boy. "Get him," he commanded. "Get him now!"

Gavin and Dillon leapt out of the car in pursuit of the young man.

TWENTY-TWO

SURPRISES ABOUND

TOMMY PUT THE BIKE in the rack, and since it didn't belong to him he left it unchained. He ran his hands over the worn tread of the tires and smiled. The rubber was really worn down. Tommy shook his head. *Man, flying was fun*, he thought, *but now it's time for business.*

Tommy stood in line and waited to enter the Mythological Artifacts Exhibit. He continuously looked over his shoulder, trying to spot the men who had kidnapped his friends. He repeatedly told himself not to be nervous, but his insides kept turning over, making it impossible.

Tommy placed his backpack on a conveyor belt for the contents to be scanned before he entered the exhibit. When he walked through the accompanying metal detector, the buzzer went off.

A large security guard pulled him to the side.

"Empty your pockets, please," he said. He produced a plastic basket for Tommy to drop in his things.

Tommy dug deep into his pockets and felt for everything, including the medallion. He put his house key, money clip, gum, lint, and the medallion in the basket. The guard ran an electronic wand up and down Tommy's body and casually glanced in the basket.

"Here," the guard said, handing back the basket. Tommy grabbed his belongings and put them back in his pockets.

"Interesting medallion."

Tommy gave the guard a strange look, surprised the man had noticed. "Yeah, I made it at school."

"You know, we have a display with those same kinds of pieces right over there." The guard pointed toward the exhibit.

Tommy didn't want to be rude. "Thank you," he said, and continued on. He tried to blend in with the groups of people wandering around the room, but none were headed in his direction. He finally latched on to a large family and walked with them as they approached the medallion display.

Tommy stared at the medallions, which were lined up in perfect rows on the blue felt blanket. He searched and compared until he found the one that resembled his. He couldn't believe how accurate the replica looked, all the way down to the same strange markings.

For a moment, Tommy felt relaxed as he gazed at the fake medallions. He smiled to himself, amazed at how much trouble this small artifact had caused.

Tommy glanced over his shoulder and his smile disappeared. He saw Gavin and Dillon making their way through the crowd.

Tommy froze. What should I do? he thought. Running seemed like a good idea, but to where?

As Gavin and Dillon drew closer, Tommy placed the real medallion on the felt display and pocketed the replica.

"What did you just do?" An older, round lady wearing a gypsy outfit approached Tommy.

"Did you just take something?" She examined the display.

"No," Tommy said.

"Are you interested in these medallions? They have tremendous stories to tell."

"You're not kidding." Tommy let out a slight laugh.

While the lady began her speech, Tommy scanned the crowd again but couldn't locate Gavin or Dillon.

"Where were they?" he wondered aloud.

"I'm sorry," he added hastily to the woman. "I've got to go."

The woman frowned. "You can come back."

Tommy saw an exit and started toward it, trying to cut through the masses. He stepped in front of a small family only to find Gavin and Dillon blocking his path.

Tommy panicked and turned to run away, but slammed into an older gentleman. Tommy lost his balance and fell to the floor. He looked up and the old man smiled at him.

"Careful, el chico," he puffed in a heavily accented voice.

Tommy scrambled to his feet, said a quick apology, and started for a different exit. He noticed men in dark suits and sunglasses appearing at every turn.

Tommy moved through a group of kids and once again ran into the same elderly gentleman.

The old man smiled. "I believe you have something we want."

Tommy looked at him in confusion. "What are you talking about? Who are you?"

"Tommy!" A familiar voice cut through the crowd. "Tommy!"

The old man and Tommy both turned to find Jack and Elizabeth waving their arms at them.

"Get away from him," Jack yelled.

Tommy's eyes fixed on the old man, who glared back at him. Tommy turned to run, but Gavin and Dillon grabbed him before he could move.

"You're not going anywhere," Gavin said as Tommy struggled to break free from his iron grip.

"Get him out of here," Manuel said.

"What about those two?"

"Not our concern." Manuel pointed in the direction of a nearby exit.

Jack and Elizabeth knocked over several people in an attempt to get to Tommy and Manuel before they left.

"The far exit, Jack," Elizabeth yelled.

As Jack reached the door, three men in dark suits tackled him to the ground. The treasure hunter bucked and rolled, jumping to his feet just as the three men grabbed for him. Jack turned to the exit when another man came through a crowd of people and jumped on him, driving him into the door.

More people gathered around as the melee continued. Parents tried to shield their kids' eyes as the fight smashed into exhibits and knocked over displays.

Elizabeth joined the fray and proceeded to kick her assailant in the stomach before landing a ferocious blow to the face. She continued her assault on two other men, who both caught direct kicks in the stomach. She thrust each of them into a concrete wall before they fell to the floor, unconscious.

Three Civic Center security men rushed in and tried to calm things, but Jack bullied his way through them.

"Come on," Jack said. He and Elizabeth ran to the side exit door. "It's locked." He tried to turn the handle.

"Front door," Elizabeth said.

The two ran toward the front of the building. Pushing open the glass doors, they saw Manuel's car speeding down the street.

"Where is our car?" Elizabeth asked.

"On the other side of the building." Jack watched the Benz disappear.

"We were so close," Elizabeth said.

"Unfortunately, that isn't good enough."

About twenty feet away, standing in the front entrance, Slider stood still, ignoring the chaos around him. He pulled out his cellphone and pushed a button.

"Yes," he said. "I see them. You are in the clear. I will meet you back at the warehouse." Slider slipped the phone back in his pocket.

"I'll deal with you later, Jack," Slider muttered to himself as he walked away, smiling at the wreckage the small ruckus had caused.

TWENTY-THREE

TWO MEDALLIONS

THE DAMP SMELL FROM the warehouse caused Chris and Jackson to sneeze repeatedly, their eyes watering. Their allergies kicked in furiously, and they couldn't stop their running noses. The Club members tried to loosen the ropes wrapped around their ankles and wrists, but found them to be tied too tight. Four large men in blue suits stood guard by them.

"Well, at least we're on a real adventure." Chris sniffed hard.

"This isn't exactly what I had in mind," Tommy said.

"You said you saw your Uncle Jack?" Shannon asked.

"I did. He was at the exhibit, but Gavin and Dillon grabbed me first."

"Be quiet," one of the large men said. "You are not supposed to talk."

"Sorry," Jackson said.

One of the guards nudged the other. "What are we waiting for?"

"Mr. Ernesto."

Manuel finally emerged from behind a curtain wearing a black robe with red markings on each breast pocket and up and down the sleeves. He moved slowly, almost trying to show off the outfit to the Club.

"Nice look," Shannon said.

"Yeah." Tommy held in a laugh. "Not many people can pull the whole warped, demented, wanna-be, evil pope thing, but you make it work."

Manuel smiled. "I'm sorry we were in such a rush at the exhibit that I didn't properly introduce myself. My name is Manuel de la Ernesto. And you are Tommy Reed, nephew of the famous Diamond Jack Reed."

"Yes," Tommy said, "you know him?"

"Of course. As a matter of fact, the reason you are in this predicament is because of him. If he had simply kept that medallion instead of sending it to you, things would be quite different."

"What makes the medallion so special?"

"And you are?"

"Jackson Miller."

"Well, Jackson Miller, it is not one medallion that is special on its own, but when you put that one medallion with a certain other one, well . . ." Manuel stopped as he realized how special the moment was to him. "It is something great."

"How do you know?"

"Good question, Mr. Reed. I see you have your uncle's inquisitive nature. The story goes back over three hundred years—1712, to be exact. In the Port Royal

161

Harbor of Jamaica, a terrible hurricane wiped out the port. At least thirty-eight vessels were destroyed."

"I know this story," Tommy said. "It was one of the greatest disasters to ever happen to Port Royal Harbor. Many people lost their lives, and homes and businesses were ruined."

"Yes, all that is true, but you don't know what happened to some of the people," Manuel said. "See, during the storm, a gypsy woman named Maria, who belonged to a secret society called the Leois, considered to be followers of the light, stole the medallion from a group called the Dorcha. The Dorcha, wanting peace, desperately needed the medallion and went after Maria."

"Who are the Dorcha?" Jackson whispered to Shannon.

"Followers of the dark," Shannon said. "I read about them in one of the reference books. But he's lying; they were not for peace of any kind. Their leaders were evil, disgusting men who would lie, cheat, steal, and kill to get what they wanted. One book said they are extinct."

"Silence when I speak!" Manuel yelled.

"I beg to differ," Jackson said out of the corner of his mouth.

"As I was saying, the Dorcha knew that whoever controlled the medallions would become all powerful and might possibly destroy the other."

"Then why didn't the gypsy woman just put the two medallions together and let the Leois destroy the Dorcha?" Shannon asked.

"Because she feared, as did her followers, that no group should be that powerful, not even her own. Pitiful woman! She sacrificed herself and threw the Leois medallion into the Caribbean Sea."

"Which is how you got my uncle involved," Tommy said matter-of-factly. "To dredge them up."

"He is the best, Tommy. Now, if you don't mind, this talk has started to bore me and I have so many more things to do."

Manuel stepped away from his prisoners, took out his medallion, and admired it for a moment. From his other pocket, he pulled out Tommy's. Just before he put them together, he said, "Watch as I bring the powers of light and dark together to achieve ultimate power."

He placed one medallion on the other and slid them together so they linked. Shannon, Chris, and Jackson closed their eyes. Tommy waited for Manuel's reaction. He noticed the guards taking several steps back toward the exit door.

But nothing happened.

Manuel pulled the medallions apart and put them back together again.

Still nothing.

Manuel looked at each medallion. Everything appeared normal. He examined Tommy's medallion closer, his eyes focusing on some small print on one of its sides.

It read, "Made in Taiwan."

Manuel exploded in anger.

"You switched them!" he screamed, storming toward Tommy. "You little . . ." He slapped Tommy across

163

the face with his open hand. "Did you think I wouldn't notice?"

The slap stunned Tommy, but he'd taken harder hits from his father and knew he could take it from Manuel too. He could still hear his uncle's voice in his head telling him to make a statement.

"The medallion isn't yours," Tommy said through clenched teeth.

Manuel glared at Tommy and breathed deeply, his anger slowly dissipating as he calmed himself.

"Did you put the real one in the exhibit?" Manuel asked.

Tommy didn't say anything.

Manuel nodded. "Your silence speaks volumes." He stood within inches of Tommy's face. "Tonight you will get the real one back."

"In exchange for my friends' release, gladly."

"I was thinking more in terms of their lives," Manuel said, "and yours."

Before Tommy could respond, he was interrupted by a new arrival.

"He's right, you know," Slider said, entering the room. "I do admire your moxie, young Tommy Reed, nephew of the great Diamond Jack Reed. Adventure must run in the genes, along with dishonesty and deception."

Tommy eyed Slider suspiciously. "How do you know my uncle?"

"Oh, he and I go way back." Slider pulled a chair closer to Tommy and the group. "So all of you want to be treasure hunters? Tough business, especially when people steal from you."

"Someone stole from you?" Chris asked.

"The great treasure hunter did." Slider smiled. "Diamond Jack himself came in and stole the cache which would have made me famous."

"I'm sure he didn't mean to," Shannon said.

Slider smiled again. "Yes he did, dear. You see, men like Jack Reed have trouble losing, and when I had him beat, he stole."

"My uncle would never do that."

Slider shook his head. "You have misplaced trust, my dear boy. Do you really think Jack Reed is in the treasure hunting business for anything other than the money?"

"He's in it for the history," Tommy seethed.

"Is that what he told you? Then you are as dumb as I thought you were smart. Diamond Jack is about himself and no one else."

"Why do you really care?" Chris asked.

"Because tonight, he and I will have a very fine reunion."

"He doesn't even know where we are," Tommy said.

"But he will, or he isn't as good as I remembered."

Slider got up and walked over to Manuel. "Get the men in position. I will do what needs to be done when Jack arrives."

"What about the woman, Elizabeth?" Manuel asked.

"Two for the price of one. Not a problem." Slider turned back to the young treasure hunters. "I am sorry that this is farewell, but I am sure we will see each other again soon."

Slider picked up the large duffel bag and walked out the door.

☆　　　☆　　　☆

Jack Reed stared at his beer and watched the foam fade. He hated losing. The uncomfortable feeling of defeat gnawed at him, causing his anger to rise.

"The whole thing is my fault," Jack said. "If I hadn't sent him that stupid medallion we would have a ton of dough, my crew would be alive, and Tommy would be out of danger."

"You didn't know that Manuel was such a bad guy." Elizabeth sipped her fruit juice as she tried to cheer up Jack.

He shrugged and took a swig of beer.

Elizabeth felt sorry for Jack, and that was new. He'd always been so sure of himself, and now, she hardly recognized him.

"We'll find Tommy."

"Where? Do you have any ideas I haven't thought of?"

Elizabeth heard the frustration in Jack's voice. He had never before doubted himself, she thought. She always saw him as the great adventurer and, for the first time, Elizabeth saw Jack as human instead of Superman.

"Let's retrace our steps," she said.

"Why?"

"Maybe there's a clue we passed over, or something we missed because of the fight."

"There sure did seem to be a lot of people helping Manuel." Jack finished his beer and ordered another.

"Maybe they were meant as a distraction?"

"Could be," Jack said, suddenly interested in the conversation. "Okay, walk me through it."

Elizabeth put down her drink. "When we got to the Civic Center, we saw Manuel and Tommy. They looked right at us, but it seemed like we'd interrupted their conversation. They had to be discussing the medallion."

"So far you've stated the obvious."

"When we ran after them, we went by the other exhibits and displays, and one of them was a big table filled with replica medallions."

"So?"

"What if Tommy saw Manuel's guys and switched the medallions?"

Jack leaned back in his chair, deep in thought.

"No way," he said. "You're stretching it, Elizabeth. I mean, even we didn't think of that. So I doubt Tommy did. He's a smart kid, but not that smart."

"You said yourself he thinks well on his feet, and what better place to make the switch? He knows it's going to be guarded. Besides, those fake FBI guys were the ones who grabbed him."

Jack quickly retraced everything in his mind. Could Tommy have hidden the medallion in plain sight? It might be the perfect place, Jack figured.

"We've got to get back to that exhibit." "It's closed now," Elizabeth said.

"Doesn't matter. If Tommy did make the switch, then Manuel is going to want it back tonight. We go now."

As he stepped in front of her, Elizabeth saw the old swagger back in Jack's walk. Elizabeth knew he didn't like to lose, which was one of the things she liked most about him.

TWENTY-FOUR

MYTH MEETS REALITY IN THE CIVIC CENTER

THE CAR PULLED UP outside of the Civic Center just before midnight. Gavin and Manuel waited for the signal to proceed as Tommy, his hands bound, stared out the window. He couldn't help but think of his Uncle Jack and hope he would show up.

A side door opened, and a ray of light broke through the darkness.

"They're in," Gavin said. The large man pulled out a knife and cut Tommy's ropes.

Manuel handed the fake medallion to Tommy. "We'll follow you in. Replace this one with the original."

Tommy got out of the car and started to walk toward the door.

"Don't think about taking off," Manuel said, reading Tommy's mind. "If you do, your friends will pay the ultimate price."

Tommy stopped and looked at Manuel, who pointed across the street to a brown van. In the windows, Tommy could see the faces of Jackson, Shannon, and Chris. Knowing any move would be fruitless, Tommy continued to the side door and walked inside. The door swung closed behind him.

One of Manuel's hulking men stood at the far end of the corridor and waved the group to move forward.

As they walked, Gavin whispered to Manuel, "Sir, why don't we just steal this thing?"

"Because according to the Dorcha code, the current holder of the medallion must give it to another or the magic will not work."

"Even under duress?"

"For the Dorcha, that's even better," Manuel said with a smile.

Gavin nodded, pretending to understand.

Three more men joined the group. The leader, a bald, heavyset individual, explained what his team had done.

"We did as you have asked, Mr. Ernesto. The security cameras are off, and all silent laser security measures have also been eliminated."

"Good work," Manuel said.

Tommy stood by himself, amazed at how large and a little frightening the exhibit looked with no people walking around.

"Go and replace the medallion," Manuel commanded.

Tommy hesitated, and then started a slow walk toward the medallion display.

He stood facing all the fake medallions, his eyes darting around the display. When he found the one he was looking for, he picked it up and flipped the fake one onto the other medallions. Tommy held the real medallion tightly and wished he could become invisible again, but this time the magic did not work.

As he started back toward Manuel, Tommy felt the need to make one last attempt to try and save the medallion and his friends. He ran to the case that held Thor's hammer and knocked it over, shattering the glass all over the floor. The famous mallet hit the ground with a loud clang. Tommy waited for the alarms to blare, but he only heard Manuel's laughter.

Manuel walked toward Tommy, clapping his hands and smiling. "Well done, young man," he said. "You are quite the adversary, but did you really think I'd forget the alarms on the displays?"

"I guess not," Tommy said, disappointed.

"Now if you could be so kind as to hand over the medallion."

Tommy's hand loosened its grip on the medallion. "Here." He lowered his head in defeat.

"Everyone has to lose some time," Manuel said.

"Not Uncle Jack," Tommy said, almost in a whisper.

Manuel grinned. "Yes, even him. But you have provided much more excitement in this little adventure, and for that, I will reward you."

"How?"

"I will perform the ceremony in the hall with you and your friends in attendance." Manuel's voice was proud.

"Sounds terrific," Tommy said sarcastically.

"It will be. Gavin, call Dillon and have him bring in the others. I don't want them to miss a thing. Now if you will excuse me, Tommy, I must prepare."

As Manuel walked away, Tommy looked around the Civic Center. If Uncle Jack planned to show up, he'd better make it fast, Tommy thought, because this was about to get ugly.

In the upper balcony, Slider settled himself into position to view the entire exhibit floor area. He waited for the arrival of Diamond Jack Reed, possibly with more anticipation than Tommy.

No matter what Manuel said, Slider knew Jack would figure out about the switch and come to rescue Tommy.

Slider fixed the scope on his high-powered rifle and scanned the area, reveling in the moment. He would end the treasure hunter's extraordinary career and, with that, reclaim his own.

TWENTY-FIVE

TOMMY COMES THROUGH

ON THE HILL OVERLOOKING the Civic Center, Jack and Elizabeth watched as the rest of the Treasure Hunters Club were led into the building through a side door.

"We'll go in that way," Jack said.

"I don't think they're just going to let us walk right through."

"Force may be necessary." Jack grinned at her.

"I was afraid you were going to say that."

Jack and Elizabeth moved quietly through the darkness. The streets by the Civic Center were deserted with the exception of the occasional car. The streetlights gave off a weak glow, which allowed Jack and Elizabeth to approach the door undetected.

Jack turned the knob and was surprised to find it unlocked.

Elizabeth's eyes widened. "Maybe we won't need violence after all."

The words no sooner left her mouth than two men jumped at Jack. They crashed to the floor, rolling around. One man threw a right fist into Jack's side, and the treasure hunter winced in pain.

Elizabeth stepped in and threw a roundhouse kick into one of the men's knees. The crack from his knee joint echoed in the hall as the man fell. Jack turned the other man around, bent his arm behind his back, and slammed him repeatedly into the door. Both men lay on the floor, softly moaning in pain.

"Good thing you didn't want to use violence," Jack said.

Elizabeth breathed deeply. "Yeah, good thing."

Jack smiled. "Use this." He pulled a rope from inside his leather coat and handed it to Elizabeth. "Tie them up and we'll put them outside."

✻   ✻   ✻

Dillon led his three young prisoners through the exhibits and over to Tommy. Dillon waved to Gavin, who nodded.

"Hey," Tommy said glumly to his friends.

They nodded, not smiling.

"What's going on? Why are we here?" Shannon asked Tommy.

"He's got the two medallions, and he wants to show us what happens when they are put together."

"What does happen?" Chris asked.

"Not sure. But my guess is that he's going to have some new power. Maybe he can just make himself invisible or something. I don't know, but I don't think it's going to be good."

"That's comforting."

"Stop talking," Dillon said. "Mr. Ernesto needs quiet."

Dillon walked over to stand beside Gavin, and they both waited for Manuel to reappear.

174

Moments later, Manuel entered the room wearing the same black robe with red trim he had worn in the warehouse. He walked to the center of the great hall and stood.

"I have waited a long time for this," he began. "Three hundred years since that gypsy woman took away what rightfully belonged to the Dorcha. Now I will avenge the dark warriors and combine the powers of light and dark for eternal and unwavering power."

"I don't know what's about to happen," Tommy said, "but I don't plan to watch it." He slammed his eyes shut.

The others did not.

"I want to see this," Jackson said.

"Me too," Chris agreed. "Shannon?"

She didn't answer. The strongest member of the Treasure Hunters Club bit her bottom lip and trembled. Her eyes welled with tears, and she could not stop staring at Manuel.

Manuel gently locked the medallions together. He wrapped both his hands around them and closed his eyes. Thunder roared and lightning flashed through the darkened windows of the Civic Center as Manuel raised his hands in the air. Deafening screams rang out through the great hall, causing everyone to wince and Chris and Jackson to shut their eyes as fear enveloped them like a blanket.

Manuel began to convulse and shake. He staggered and fell to his knees. The medallion shot red and blue lights

175

across the Civic Center that refracted off the displays and mirrors.

In one moment, two beams came together and slammed into Manuel, who screamed as the blast raised him off the floor and put him on the ground.

Then there was quiet.

Tommy opened his eyes slowly and came face-to-face with a horrifying sight. Manuel, once an elderly man, had been transformed into an eight-foot-tall demon, with red eyes and glowing orange fingertips.

"Oh, my," Shannon said. "I don't think that the power to become invisible is all he'll get."

"What happened to him?" Chris asked, stunned.

"He's going to kill us," Jackson said.

"The power," Manuel breathed, "I can feel it pulsing through my body." He raised his bony and gnarled hands in the air. Fire shot from his fingertips, shattering display boxes and statues. "The ultimate power," he growled.

He walked toward the youngsters and waved a finger at Dillon.

"Unbind them," he roared.

Dillon and Gavin stared at their former boss, unable to move.

"Now!" the demon screamed.

Dillon ran over and cut the kids loose. The Club members stood together, just staring at the beast, unsure of what to do next.

"It is time for all of you to be dealt with," Manuel said.

He raised the locked medallions above his head and started to chant something in an unrecognizable language.

Terrified, Jackson stuttered, "A-a-any ideas?"

"No." Shannon backed up into Tommy.

"I never thought we'd go out like this," Chris said.

"We won't." Tommy pointed toward the Roman display. "Look!"

Everyone, including Manuel, turned and saw Jack Reed holding the bow used by Diana, the Roman goddess of hunting, raised and ready.

Jack released two arrows, which struck Manuel's disfigured hand. The medallions fell to the ground as the demon screamed in pain.

"Get them!" Jack yelled, dropping the bow and running toward the medallions.

The medallions slid across the floor, and a mad scramble followed in pursuit of them.

Jack's hand reached out to grab the medallions, but Gavin tackled him and the two men rolled across the floor. Dillon tried to catch the medallions only to find Elizabeth's foot connecting with his face, knocking him backward.

Elizabeth lunged for the medallions, but was sideswiped by a recovered Dillon as they rolled over one another.

Tommy ran to the medallions, but Manuel, after pulling the arrows from his hand, took a quick step forward and slapped Tommy off his feet. Tommy skidded into the medallion table, scattering the replicas along the floor.

When Tommy looked up, he saw Shannon pulling Dillon off Elizabeth followed by his uncle's assistant planting two quick kicks to Dillon's face. He fell forward, unconscious.

Chris and Jackson started toward the medallions. As they reached them, Manuel's large arm crashed down in front of them, shattering the floor. The two boys toppled into one another and ended up on the ground.

Gavin, meanwhile, held Jack down and threw successive punches at him. Jack responded with two quick shots, eventually rolling over Gavin and gaining the advantage and putting his adversary out of commission.

As Jack rose, the sound of a sinister and evil laugh echoed throughout the hall.

"Looking for this?" growled Manuel, holding up the medallions.

"You've looked better, Manuel," Jack said as he and the others turned their attention to the large demon. "I mean, I've heard of people letting themselves go, but this is ridiculous."

"You are not looking all that good yourself."

"I haven't been working out like I should," Jack said.

"Jack, you should have found this treasure and given it to me quietly. You would have had the money, without problems."

"True," Jack agreed.

"That was all you were looking for, wasn't it? The big payday. You didn't care about the treasure or the history. It was only about the money."

Tommy and the others looked on in disbelief. They didn't believe what they were hearing could be true.

Jack looked at Tommy and the young treasure hunters he'd inspired and saw the pained expressions on their faces. He knew he'd let them down.

"There was a time when that happened, but it's in the past," Jack said. "Now hand over the two medallions."

"Sorry, Jack, but I have waited far too long for this."

Jack stared at Manuel, gazing deeply into his red eyes. As if through a looking glass, Jack saw directly into Manuel's evil and despicable soul filled with nothing but anger, greed, deception, and murder.

"You were there three hundred years ago during that hurricane," he said. "You chased the woman into the harbor. That's how you knew where the medallion was and that there were two of them."

Manuel smiled, and his large fangs dripped with white, sticky saliva. "I was, Jack, and the gypsy woman Maria thought she could hide them, but she couldn't. She didn't know the power of the Dorcha. I waited patiently, and now the power is mine."

"Not for long!" Tommy yelled, and slammed one of the Vajras—a thunderbolt scepter—into Manuel's muscular thigh. The force of the blow knocked the scepter out of Tommy's hands, leaving him defenseless.

"You shouldn't have done that!" Manuel screamed, swinging his large claw at Tommy and battering him in the chest.

Chris ran at Manuel and leapt at the demon's stomach, his fists out, but it felt like hitting a brick wall. Chris flailed backward, crashing into the Zeus display.

Shannon and Jackson ran for Tommy and pushed him out of the way as the demon's claw pounded the ground, cracking the marble floor as the medallions slid away.

Tommy rolled toward the medallions and grabbed them, but the heat from their combined power sent a burning shockwave up his arm. Tommy immediately let go of the medallions and tried to cover his hand beneath his shirt to dull the pain, but it didn't work. His hand had already started to blister.

Manuel proceeded to slap around the rest of the Club members like they were rag dolls. He took a swipe at Elizabeth and leveled her to the ground. Then he walked slowly toward Jack and stood glaring over him.

"It's over, Diamond Jack," Manuel hissed.

"Tommy," Jack yelled. "No matter what happens, destroy the medallions."

Jack slipped away just as Manuel's claw smashed another deep hole into the floor. Jack was unable to get to his feet. Manuel continued his assault as Jack ducked and rolled away.

Tommy looked around for something to smash the medallions with and spotted Thor's hammer. Without

180

thinking, he grabbed the famous mallet with two hands and raised it above his head, then swung it down hard on the medallions.

When the hammer connected, the medallions shattered into tiny pieces, causing a seismic blast that spared no one with its power. In the balcony, Slider was lifted off his feet and thrown back against the wall.

Hundreds of blue and red streaks of light shot around the room. Each one raced through Manuel, who tried desperately to stand as he absorbed blow after blow that finally forced him to his knees.

The last of the beams slammed into Manuel's chest and he slumped to the ground; his body transformed from demon back to a battered and burned old man.

Jack ran to Tommy. "Are you all right?" he asked, helping his nephew to his feet.

"Yeah. Where are the others?"

Tommy and Jack helped the rest of the Treasure Hunters Club and Elizabeth to their feet.

"Is everybody okay?" Jack asked.

They all nodded in the affirmative.

"Is it over?" Shannon asked.

Tommy turned and saw the moaning and crying Manuel de la Ernesto, a shell of what he once was. "I think so."

"Good," Chris said. "I want to go home."

"Me too," Jackson added.

Elizabeth leaned on Jack and closed her eyes.

"Is she going to be all right?" Tommy asked.

"Just a few bumps and bruises. What do you say we get out of here and call the police?"

Jack pulled out his cellphone and dialed 911.

"Can you believe what we just saw?" Shannon said in amazement.

"That might be one of the grossest things I have ever witnessed," Chris added.

"I think I've seen it all." Jackson smiled. "It's good to be treasure hunters."

The first shot ricocheted off the ground and sounded like a firecracker.

"Was that a gun-shot?" Tommy asked.

Three more blasts erupted, and the group scrambled behind anything they could find for protection.

"Is everyone all right?" Elizabeth yelled.

"I don't think so." Jack turned toward Tommy, who could see the red blood. "I got hit in the arm."

"How bad? Are you okay?" Tommy asked.

Jack bit his lip. "God, it burns."

"Who is shooting at us?" Elizabeth screamed.

As the shots continued, Tommy remembered the man from the warehouse. "Is it that Slider guy?" he yelled out.

Jack's eyes narrowed, the pain in his arm subsiding for a moment. "Did you say 'Slider'?"

"Yeah." Tommy nodded.

Elizabeth saw the look on Jack's face. "Jack, what is it?"

"Tommy, you've got to take this man out," Jack said.

Tommy looked at his uncle incredulously. "I can't do that. I'm just a kid."

"First off, calm down and get ahold of yourself." Jack's voice was calm. "Second, you can do this, but more importantly, you have to or else we won't get out of this alive."

Tommy stared at his uncle's pleading eyes and saw the others doing the same. They were looking to him. He couldn't—wouldn't—let them down.

"All right." Tommy took a deep breath.

He looked up from behind his barricade and saw what he needed.

"We've got your back," Shannon said.

Tommy nodded confidently and waited for just the right moment before sprinting toward the display holding David's famous slingshot and Achilles' shield. Tommy grabbed the replica shield and hid behind it as he slid the leather sling and rock in his pocket. He made his way to the upper balcony, pushing the heavy relic shield up one step at a time.

Slider reloaded and saw the moving target. He fired rapidly, shell casings hitting the floor with every squeeze of the trigger. Each shot bounced off the gleaming shield.

Another pause in the firing allowed Tommy to pull the slingshot from his pocket. It was exactly like the one David used to defeat Goliath. Tommy loaded the stone and waited. As soon as he saw Slider's face, Tommy swung the sling above his head and let the rock fly.

The stone struck Slider just above his right eye, drawing blood and staggering him.

Slider found his footing and stood up for his nemesis to see.

"I've waited a long time for this, Jack, and you send a boy?"

"He's probably better than both of us, Slider."

"He's not the one I want, Jack. It's you!" Slider spat.

"I figured you'd be doing something like this now. How much is Manuel paying you?" Jack tried to egg Slider on.

"It's not about the money," Slider said. "This is about revenge. You stole my life!"

"I did not." Jack dismissed the comment. "You were never that good to begin with because the history meant nothing to you and you lacked patience."

Slider raised his rifle and peered through the scope. "I seem to have gotten over that." Slider's finger felt the trigger, and he saw Jack's head in his crosshairs. "Say goodbye, Diamond Jack."

"No!" Shannon yelled, and flung an Aboriginal boomerang at Slider. The wooden weapon spun in an arch through the air and hit the barrel of the rifle, throwing the shot off. The bullet drove harmlessly into the wall.

Before Slider could gather himself for another try, he heard sirens blaring in the distance. He quickly stuffed the gun in his duffle bag and headed for the rooftop exit, not bothering to look back.

Slider entered the stairway and started climbing the four flights up to the roof of the Civic Center.

There will be another time for Jack Reed, Slider promised himself, and for those kids.

Definitely another time.

TWENTY-SIX

AFTERMATH

TOMMY WALKED BACK TO the others. He let the open sling dangle at his side and wore a smile on his face.

"You guys can come out now."

"Who was that?" Chris asked as he stood and dusted off his clothes.

"An old friend." Jack pushed himself up.

"How's your arm?" Tommy asked.

"Hurts, but I don't think any major damage was done."

"Jack, do all your old friends shoot at you?" Shannon asked.

"Just the ones who don't turn into demons," Jack quipped.

Elizabeth limped over and leaned heavily on Jackson's shoulder.

"Can you please explain that?" she asked.

"He was a treasure hunter a long time ago and he," Jack paused, unsure of what to say about Slider. "He lost his way."

"So he tried to kill you?" Elizabeth said.

"Something like that."

186

"I've known you for a long time, Jack, and I know there's more to this story than what you're telling me."

"Elizabeth, trust me, it's not worth talking about," Jack said. "Where'd Tommy go?"

Tommy stood by Manuel before kneeling down next to him. Manuel remained curled up in a ball on the floor, tears streaming from his eyes.

"Are you all right?" Tommy asked.

Manuel's words made no sense, and Tommy looked at the others for help. Jack and Elizabeth approached and, as they saw what their former employer had become, sad expressions crept across their faces.

In the distance, sirens grew closer.

"Come on, Tommy," Jack said. "He's lost now."

"What's wrong with him?"

"The powers of light and dark are supposed to be separated. That way no one can abuse them. Manuel didn't see that." Jack shook his head. "He didn't realize that when the powers are combined, it is too much for one person. No human can control all of that power. Not even a Dorcha. That's why the Leois put the power into two medallions and gave them to the gypsies to hide. They are meant to be apart."

"Thanks to Tommy, no one is going to have that power again," Chris said.

"Thor's hammer really does work." Tommy smiled.

"Tommy," Jack said, and looked around at the others, "all of you did a great job. You risked your lives to protect a friend and historical artifacts. As a treasure hunter, I couldn't be prouder of you."

The main doors of the Civic Center burst open and a flood of policemen came through, guns out and ready.

"Show your hands," Jack said. "Let's not give them a reason to shoot one of us."

"Don't move," a young officer called.

"We are unarmed." Jack raised his good arm in the air. "The people you want are in the exhibit and on the side of the building."

Several policemen rushed by the group and saw Gavin and Dillon, beaten and unconscious, and a hysterical, babbling Manuel.

Four policemen brought in two other men from a distant hallway and gathered them together.

"Who is responsible for all of this?" a large man in a tan trench coat asked.

"Go ahead, Tommy, tell him," Jack said.

"I guess I am, sir."

"I'm Detective Converse," the man said. "Can you explain to me what happened here tonight?"

"Sure." Tommy began recounting the entire tale for the detective.

✳   ✳   ✳

Slider's boots made soft pinging noises as he scaled the metal stairs to the Civic Center rooftop. He pushed open the emergency exit door and jogged out onto the tarred roof.

The numerous lights from the police cars lit up the neighborhood in blues and reds as he made his way to the far side of the building. With no other way out, Slider jumped the thirty feet down to the soft ground. He hit the grassy hill and rolled on impact.

His training allowed him to take the fall without serious injury. He limped his way through four alleyways toward a parked BMW.

He got in the car, turned the key in the ignition, and drove away, his taillights disappearing into the darkness.

✻   ✻   ✻

After half an hour, Detective Converse stared at Tommy in disbelief. "I've never heard anything like that in my life," the gritty policeman said.

Suddenly, an older gentleman came through the front doors. Tommy and the other treasure hunters recognized him immediately.

"It's Mr. Thornberry, the director of the exhibit," Tommy said.

"Officer, oh my God, Officer." Thornberry spotted the damage to the displays. "Who is responsible for this? I want them arrested and put in jail immediately. Is it Tommy and his Club friends?"

"Sir," Converse said, "if you could just settle down a bit, I can explain. I think."

Thornberry had run the Exhibit for Mythological Artifacts for over twenty years and never before heard as wild a story as the one Converse told him about the medallions. No one believed Tommy.

Thornberry looked at Tommy. "There is no way that Thor's hammer was able to destroy anything, much less gold medallions. It's a replica! They are all replicas."

"Well," Tommy shrugged. "It did."

"This is the most unbelievable story I have ever heard." Thornberry shook his head.

"Excuse me, Mr. Thornberry," Jack cut in. "My name is Jack Reed and I would be happy to help you replace some of the artifacts that were damaged or destroyed here this evening."

Thornberry eyed Jack. "You look familiar to me. Wait a second, are you *the* Diamond Jack Reed? Tommy's uncle?"

"One and the same," Jack said, smiling.

"I have read about you. It would be a great honor to have someone of your expertise help with this exhibit. I think we should have a talk."

"Sounds good." Jack shook Thornberry's hand and then winced. "But first I need to get to a hospital. My arm hurts a bit."

"There is an ambulance outside," Converse said.

Tommy wrapped his arm around his uncle and led him and the others out of the Civic Center to a waiting ambulance.

TWENTY-SEVEN

A HAPPY MEETING

CHRIS AND JACKSON SAT at the new rectangular oak table and couldn't help but smile.

Since the Treasure Hunters Club helped stop Manuel and his men, life had changed. Newspapers carried only the believable half of the story, which even received some national attention. People from across the country took notice and sent donations to the Treasure Hunters Club.

The first thing to arrive at the clubhouse was five new computers to replace their old one. The Club also received two laptops to help when they were traveling, not that the group traveled much. They were also given new cellphones with Internet access.

Tommy, with Uncle Jack's help, purchased new equipment for their treasure hunts. Metal detectors, sonar equipment, and new electro-analysis devices would aid the treasure hunters in the future.

The newspaper headlines, "Teen Club Thwarts Crime," were placed behind glass and hung on the walls. Each article about the group was written in the same fashion, discussing each member of the Treasure Hunters

Club and his or her role in stopping Manuel, who was described only as some kind of thief of ancient relics.

The Treasure Hunters Club received an award from the donors of the Exhibit of Mythological Artifacts for saving the exhibit and increasing the interest level in the community and the rest of the country.

"It's been two weeks, and I'm starting to miss all the action that went with the medallions," Chris said as he walked across the room and sat at a new computer.

"I'm not," Jackson said.

"Why?"

"We were almost killed by that demon-devil guy,"

"But we weren't," Chris said. "Besides, according to the reporters there is no such thing. Next time will be better."

"I don't know," Jackson said. "Why don't we just talk about lost treasure?"

"Because it's boring."

They both turned their heads to the door when it opened.

Tommy walked in with Shannon and carried a small box.

"What's in the box?" Jackson asked.

"The medallion." Tommy opened the box and pulled out the medallion.

"The medallion?" Jackson asked, puzzled. "You destroyed it."

"I know," Tommy said. "Mr. Thornberry thought I would like a replica for our treasure shelf."

Tommy held up the medallion and admired its shine and beauty.

"Okay then, let's start the meeting." Chris walked over to the group.

Tommy sat at the front of the table and put the medallion in his pocket.

"What's our next adventure?" Chris asked.

"High school," Jackson said.

"Not that one."

"Speaking of adventure, what is your Uncle Jack going to do now?" Shannon asked.

"He said he's going to take some time off. He felt really bad about the crew and how he was tricked by Manuel. He's just frustrated, I think."

"What's the deal with Manuel, anyway?" Jackson asked.

"Last I heard he was moved to some insane hospital outside of Boston. Detective Converse called and told me not to worry about him coming back."

"So what is our new adventure?" Chris asked again.

Tommy smiled. For all the times he wished he were out on the ocean or exploring some old mine shaft for treasure, the thing he loved most was his time spent with his friends. Their adventures would come, he told himself, and they would be more rewarding because they had each other.

"I say we head to the library and start with the new reference books," Tommy said.

"Good idea," Jackson agreed.

"I want an adventure." Chris crossed his arms.

"No you don't," Shannon said. "Remember that ninety percent of all treasure hunting is research. So shut it, get on your bike, and let's go to the library."

"We can stop at Lou's," Tommy said. "I'll pay for cherry ice cones."

Chris shook his head and followed Shannon and Jackson out of the clubhouse door.

Tommy stood to leave and remembered the medallion. He opened the glass case containing the Club's artifacts and looked at the new materials, each one representing their adventures. Thor's hammer, given to the Treasure Hunters Club by Mr. Thornberry, sat in the center of the case. Tommy moved aside some buffalo coins and the TAB can, then laid the medallion against the back wall.

He smiled. *What an adventure it had been*, he thought. He saw the words "Made in Taiwan" inscribed on the side of the medallion and laughed. Tommy locked the glass case and walked out the door to join the others.

"I have great friends," he said softly to himself.

THE END

About the Author

Sean Paul McCartney (He's not related to the Beatle) was born in 1971. He graduated from Alfred University in upstate New York with a Bachelor's in Communications in 1993. From there he played two exciting seasons traveling around the world with the Washington Generals playing against the world famous Harlem Globetrotters. In 1996 Sean earned his Master's in Education and embarked on a career as a teacher. He is employed by Plain Local Schools in Canton, OH. He has a beautiful wife and two children. To learn more about Sean, check out his Web site at www.sean-mccartney.com.

Made in the USA
Lexington, KY
18 October 2018